THE LOST LANGUAGE OF OYSTERS

By Alexander McCall Smith

THE NO. 1 LADIES' DETECTIVE AGENCY SERIES

The No. 1 Ladies' Detective Agency
Tears of the Giraffe
Morality for Beautiful Girls
The Kalahari Typing School for Men
The Full Cupboard of Life
In the Company of Cheerful Ladies
Blue Shoes and Happiness
The Good Husband of Zebra Drive
The Miracle at Speedy Motors
Tea Time for the Traditionally Built
The Double Comfort Safari Club
The Saturday Big Tent Wedding Party
The Limpopo Academy of Private Detection
The Minor Adjustment Beauty Salon
The Handsome Man's De Luxe Café
The Woman Who Walked in Sunshine
Precious and Grace
The House of Unexpected Sisters
The Colours of all the Cattle
To the Land of Long Lost Friends
How to Raise an Elephant
The Joy and Light Bus Company
A Song of Comfortable Chairs
From a Far and Lovely Country
The Great Hippopotamus Hotel

THE ISABEL DALHOUSIE NOVELS

The Sunday Philosophy Club
Friends, Lovers, Chocolate
The Right Attitude to Rain
The Careful Use of Compliments
The Comfort of Saturdays
The Lost Art of Gratitude
The Charming Quirks of Others
The Forgotten Affairs of Youth
The Uncommon Appeal of Clouds
The Novel Habits of Happiness
A Distant View of Everything
The Quiet Side of Passion
The Geometry of Holding Hands
The Sweet Remnants of Summer
The Conditions of Unconditional Love

THE 44 SCOTLAND STREET SERIES

44 Scotland Street
Espresso Tales
Love Over Scotland
The World According to Bertie
The Unbearable Lightness of Scones
The Importance of Being Seven
Bertie Plays the Blues
Sunshine on Scotland Street
Bertie's Guide to Life and Mothers
The Revolving Door of Life
The Bertie Project
A Time of Love and Tartan
The Peppermint Tea Chronicles
A Promise of Ankles
Love in the Time of Bertie
The Enigma of Garlic
The Stellar Debut of Galactica MacFee

THE CORDUROY MANSIONS SERIES

Corduroy Mansions
The Dog Who Came in from the Cold
A Conspiracy of Friends

THE VON IGELFELD ENTERTAINMENTS

The 2½ Pillars of Wisdom
Unusual Uses for Olive Oil
Your Inner Hedgehog

THE DETECTIVE VARG NOVELS

The Department of Sensitive Crimes
The Talented Mr Varg
The Man with the Silver Saab
The Discreet Charm of the Big Bad Wolf

La's Orchestra Saves the World
The Forever Girl
My Italian Bulldozer
The Private Life of Spies

THE LOST LANGUAGE OF OYSTERS

Alexander McCall Smith

abacus
books

ABACUS

First published in Great Britain in 2025 by Abacus

1 3 5 7 9 10 8 6 4 2

Copyright © Alexander McCall Smith 2025
Illustration copyright © Iain McIntosh 2025

The moral right of the author has been asserted.

*All characters and events in this publication, other than those
clearly in the public domain, are fictitious and any resemblance
to real persons, living or dead, is purely coincidental.*

All rights reserved.
No part of this publication may be reproduced, stored in a
retrieval system, or transmitted, in any form or by any means, without
the prior permission in writing of the publisher, nor be otherwise circulated
in any form of binding or cover other than that in which it is published
and without a similar condition including this condition being
imposed on the subsequent purchaser.

A CIP catalogue record for this book is available from the British Library.

Hardback ISBN 978-0-349-14766-6
Trade paperback ISBN 978-0-349-14767-3

Typeset in Galliard by M Rules
Printed and bound in Great Britain by Clays Ltd, Elcograf S.p.A.

Papers used by Abacus are from well-managed forests
and other responsible sources.

Abacus
An imprint of
Little, Brown Book Group
Carmelite House
50 Victoria Embankment
London EC4Y 0DZ

The authorised representative
in the EEA is
Hachette Ireland
8 Castlecourt Centre
Dublin 15, D15 XTP3, Ireland
(email: info@hbgi.ie)

An Hachette UK Company
www.hachette.co.uk

www.littlebrown.co.uk

This book is for Wolfgang Kothes
and Susanne Moll

Intriguing News from Professor Garelli-Ferrari

Moritz-Maria von Igelfeld sat back in his chair and closed his eyes. It was mid-afternoon on a sultry June day, and he could easily have dropped off to sleep, had it not been for the fact that he was at a conference, sitting in the front row, and there were seventy other people in the room. Of these seventy, at least forty, perhaps more, would have been delighted to see his head begin to nod. They would not have been charitable in any reporting of the event, unlike most of us who sympathise with those who doze off at odd times. Quite the opposite, in fact: they would have taken considerable pleasure in telling others that they had seen Professor Dr Dr (*honoris causa*) (*mult.*) Moritz-Maria von Igelfeld, author of that towering work of Romance linguistics, *Portuguese Irregular Verbs*, falling asleep in the middle of a conference.

'Right there,' they might say. 'Before our eyes. Falling asleep in the middle of the conference session.'

'You would have thought,' they might continue, 'that somebody in his position would be more careful.' And that statement would be accompanied by a knowing look, tinged with reproach, implying that von Igelfeld was perhaps beginning to slip a bit. After all, *Portuguese Irregular Verbs* had been published over a decade ago, and nobody could be expected to remain at the top of his game indefinitely ...

That is what such people might have been expected to say, and their motivation, in almost every case, would have been pure jealousy. For von Igelfeld, on his academic mountain, on the Parnassus that was *Portuguese Irregular Verbs*, had many detractors whose tents were pitched on the less fortunate plains below. None of these lesser professors, of course, had ever published anything approaching *Portuguese Irregular Verbs* in its scope and magisterial authority. It was true that some of them had produced monographs that had attracted a certain degree of attention, but none of them, von Igelfeld was confident, would have written anything with quite as many pages as his groundbreaking disquisition on irregular verbs. Of course, the length of a book was no guarantee of quality, anything but, in fact – many second-rate books were excessively prolix, sometimes prolonging the discussion of a minor point for twenty or thirty pages, without counting a lengthy coda of obscure and long-winded footnotes. In the case of *Portuguese Irregular Verbs*, however, every page earned its keep, as von Igelfeld put it, and an Occam's razor approach to footnotes had reduced the length of that particular section of the book to a mere one hundred pages.

But it was not only the status of *Portuguese Irregular Verbs* that triggered jealousy among other scholars: it was the fact that von Igelfeld's Institute in Regensburg was better funded than any other linguistics department in Germany. This was the result of a historical error made by the University as long ago as 1973, when a misplaced decimal point had resulted in the Institute of Romance Philology receiving ten times more funding than it needed. Attempts by the University to rectify the mistake the following year were met with outrage from the wider academic staff, who realised that if one department could be singled out for budgetary cuts, then none of the rest of them was safe. The cause had even attracted the attention of a faction of the Baader-Meinhoff gang, a radical terrorist group of the time, that saw in the threatened reduction of the Institute's funding a chance to pick a fight with the University, which they considered to be a pillar of the system they were seeking to overthrow. The Baader-Meinhoff warning that they would be prepared to blow up the entire University if the proposed cut in funding went ahead had been taken seriously. The University was keen to protect its staff and was in no mood for a showdown with a group that had a vivid track record of kidnapping and assassination. The whole matter was quietly dropped; the Institute continued to benefit from its over-generous funding, allowing it to offer high salaries and better conditions that any of its competitors at other German universities. It was this comfortable financial situation that enabled von Igelfeld to occupy a chair with no teaching responsibilities whatsoever, and with almost limitless funds for conference attendance.

That particular benefit had been ruthlessly exploited by one of von Igelfeld's close colleagues, Professor Dr Detlev Amadeus Unterholzer. Unterholzer, who was the author of what von Igelfeld considered to be a minor work on the subjunctive mood, never lost an opportunity to attend a conference. Not only that, but he was also known for his willingness to chair sessions, in which he had a tendency to speak at great length himself before cutting off other speakers on the grounds of limited time. Unterholzer also insisted on travelling first-class to any conference, usually taking one of the Institute's assistants (travelling second-class, admittedly) to help him with his luggage. This practice was very much disapproved of by Professor Dr Dr Florianus Prinzel, whose modest and unassuming nature precluded such profligacy. 'Our dear colleague, Professor Dr Unterholzer, is certainly not prepared to rough it,' Prinzel commented to von Igelfeld. 'I see that he is booked in to the Waldorf Astoria for that conference in New York next month.'

Von Igelfeld shook his head in a disapproving manner. 'There are some who have to make up for what they otherwise lack,' he observed. 'Dear Professor Dr Unterholzer is perhaps one such. We must be patient, though, with the weaker brethren, and their little failings.'

But patience can be hard, and now, in the conference hall, with his eyes briefly closed, von Igelfeld listened with mounting irritation to the speaker currently addressing the delegates. This was Professor Marco-Antonio Garelli-Ferrari, the holder of a Chair of Anthropological Linguistics at the *Istituto Parmese Carlo Fontanelli* and an expert in the linguistic features of very early languages, some of them so early, and so obscure, as to have left behind little or no evidence of their existence. In a previous paper that von Igelfeld had heard him delivering in Budapest, Professor Garelli-Ferrari had explained his theory, first advanced in his *A Neanderthal Suppositional Grammar*, that Neanderthal populations had developed sophisticated language, the broad details of which could be hypothesised on the basis of what was known about the earliest manifestation of language in *homo sapiens*. Now he was speculating as to their likely incipient vocabulary. 'The Neanderthal word for mother,' he suggested, 'almost certainly involved the *m* sound, just as it does in modern languages.'

Von Igelfeld opened his eyes to glance at his neighbour, who made a gesture of despair. This really was too much, he thought. There were more and more attempts to portray Neanderthals as being much more advanced than they probably were. Their few cave handprints were primitive in the extreme, and yet there were those who now talked enthusiastically about Neanderthal art as if it were no more than a step or two behind the art of Renaissance Florence.

'Ridiculous,' von Igelfeld whispered to his neighbour, adding, 'Did you see his recent article on the Sanskrit etymology of *moon*?'

The neighbour laughed. 'Some people will believe anything,' he said, adding, *sotto voce*, '*Il* Garelli-Ferrari is clearly a very dangerous man. There can be no excuse for such *lunacy*.'

This subtle joke appealed greatly to von Igelfeld, who chuckled to himself for some time afterwards. Those who said that the world of linguistics was dry and without its comic moments, were, in his view, quite unaware of the strong current of piquant humour present at conferences such as this. Etymological jokes may not be everyone's cup of tea, thought von Igelfeld, but for those with a well-tuned ear, they were small gems on the prosaic shores of life. Only last month, he himself had made a witty observation about the use of intensifiers in early French that had brought the metaphorical house down at morning coffee in the Institute. Herr Huber, the Institute's rather fussy librarian, had been so amused that he had written von Igelfeld's words down in his notebook there and then.

'You must forgive me for transcribing you so immediately, Professor von Igelfeld,' he had said as he tucked his notebook away. 'But had Mr Boswell not been ready with his pencil, then many of the remarks made by Dr Johnson would have been lost to posterity. A chronicler must always be ready to chronicle, I believe.'

Von Igelfeld had not minded at all, and was about to reassure Herr Huber of this when the Librarian, frowning slightly, launched into one of his soliloquies.

'Of course,' continued Herr Huber, 'we cannot be sure that it was a pencil that Mr Boswell used to write down Dr Johnson's *bons mots*. If he wrote them all down while they were travelling – and they did get about, those two – then I *assume* that he would have used a pencil because he could hardly have dipped his pen into ink to make entries while travelling in a coach or walking along, or whatever. A pencil, I imagine, would have been far easier. We should not forget, though, that there were those little travelling inkwells – have you seen them? – that were designed for use away from one's regular desk. They made things easier, and it's quite possible that Mr Boswell had one of those.'

Unterholzer had been present in the coffee room during this exchange, and had sighed audibly as Herr Huber made his observations about pencils. 'Quite so, Herr Huber,' he muttered. 'But does it really matter?'

That was a question that Unterholzer sometimes asked when Herr Huber regaled his colleagues with inconsequential remarks. On this occasion, von Igelfeld sprang to the Librarian's defence. 'It can matter a great deal, Professor Dr Unterholzer,' he said. 'Pencils lack the permanency of ink. Of course, whether *that* matters depends on whether what is written down is worth preserving. Not everything is. There are some books, for example, that are allowed to go out of print when the first printing is exhausted. I am not talking about any books in particular, I must point out ... '

He *was* talking about a particular book, of course, and the reference was immediately picked up by all those present. Unterholzer's two-volume treatise on the subjunctive had been duly reprinted a couple of years after first publication, but the same could not be said of his earlier book on vowel shifts. That had been allowed to go out of print only a year after first publication – a fact that von Igelfeld occasionally referred to – indirectly, of course – and that still rankled with Unterholzer himself.

Unterholzer glowered, but said nothing. Herr Huber, who was careful not to take sides in academic disputes, quickly diverted the conversation. 'There is a nurse in my aunt's nursing home who always carries a propelling pencil,' he began. 'She is a very highly qualified person from Westphalia, I believe. That always makes me think of the Peace of Westphalia, by the way – you know how we associate one thing with another? Anyway, that's where she's from – Münster, I think, although I may be wrong about that. She has a rather beautiful silver propelling pencil that she uses when she is making notes on patients' charts. It was given to her by an uncle of hers who has a stationery shop. It was for her twenty-first birthday. I can always tell when she has written something on my aunt's chart because I recognise the pencil entry. And her handwriting is exemplary, I must say.'

Von Igelfeld stifled a yawn. Herr Huber meant well – everybody acknowledged that – but there was an overwhelming inconsequentiality to so much of what he said. 'Well . . .' he began.

He did not get far. 'She says,' Herr Huber continued, 'that the manager of the nursing home sometimes tells her that a pen entry would be preferable, but she tells me that she ignores him. She is the one who arranged for my aunt to be put on a different pill recently for her blood pressure, you see. You don't want too much pressure, but you don't want it to be too low either. It's difficult. It's rather like coffee, I think: you don't want it to be too hot, but cold coffee is undrinkable, I find. Of course, it was the manager who arranged the new pill, not the nurse. Although it wasn't really the manager who made the decision – it was the doctor. He's not always there, you see . . .'

'Very interesting, Herr Huber,' said von Igelfeld quickly, looking at his watch. 'But time marches on, doesn't it?'

*

Polite applause followed Professor Garelli-Ferrari's paper, with only a few signs of a more enthusiastic response, all of which came from his colleagues from Parma, who were sitting in the front row. Von Igelfeld was courteous, of course, and applauded dutifully, but with a pained expression that left no doubt as to his real feelings. Poor Garelli-Ferrari, he thought – to be so misguided about so much, and yet to be completely unaware of it. Mind you, he told himself, most, if not all, misguided people remained ignorant of their misunderstandings and errors – Garelli-Ferrari's attitude was nothing remarkable in that context. And in Garelli-Ferrari's defence, von Igelfeld reminded himself, was the fact that he was Italian, and most Italians were misguided in some respect or another, except, of course, in those northerly areas of the country, such as Bolzano, where people spoke German rather than Italian. Italians were charming people, he felt, but rather excitable in a tight corner, or in any corner, in fact.

Leaving the conference hall, von Igelfeld made his way to the bar area, where coffee was served during the break between sessions. A cup of coffee, he thought, would help him to remain awake through the afternoon's remaining papers, of which he saw there were to be two. The naming theme was to be continued with a presentation by an Australian professor on the use of multiple personal names in a remote language community in New Guinea. That could be interesting, von Igelfeld thought, and such papers were surely due to become less common, given the declining numbers speaking obscure New Guinea languages. Yet there would still be papers to write, as increasing cohorts of anthropologists living with the remaining speakers meant that a whole new category of loan-words had been identified and in due course would require study. *Data, transcript* and *reportage* were now words in common usage in those remote highlands, and in some areas the most widely used word for *stranger* was now *anthropologist*. The meaning of loan-words can, of course, change. In New Guinea, *data* is used for a particular sort of yam, and *reportage* is used to describe the sound made when one clears one's throat on getting up in the morning.

He found a seat away from the main cluster of conference-goers and took the first few sips of his coffee. A few minutes later he noticed that Professor Garelli-Ferrari had emerged from a side-door and was surveying the delegates. It did not take him long to spot von Igelfeld and to make his way over to join him.

'*Chiarissimo professore*,' he said, reaching out to shake von Igelfeld's hand.

Von Igelfeld bowed his head. 'Professor Cavaliere Garelli-Ferrari,' he said. 'That was a most interesting paper.'

Garelli-Ferrari beamed, both at the use of his title, *cavaliere*, and the complimenting of his paper. 'You were persuaded?' he asked.

Von Igelfeld looked away. 'It was an intriguing hypothesis.'

'But it was one that you would be prepared to support?' Garelli-Ferrari pressed.

'In part,' answered von Igelfeld. It was always possible to agree with *something* in any paper, even if the major premisses on which it was based were untenable.

Garelli-Ferrari seemed relieved. 'That is most gratifying,' he said. 'I was most grateful to your colleague, Professor Dr Unterholzer, for reading an earlier version. He made some very helpful suggestions.'

Von Igelfeld stared fixedly ahead. This did not surprise him: Unterholzer would read *anything*, he decided, and was most undiscriminating in his willingness to consider outrageous theories.

'But enough about me,' said Garelli-Ferrari, lowering himself uninvited onto the chair next to von Igelfeld's. 'We should talk about you, dear Professor von Igelfeld. You have been in my mind recently.'

Von Igelfeld waited. He could not imagine why Garelli-Ferrari should think of him when there were pressing issues of Neanderthal grammar to consider.

'You will have seen the new book published by my dear former colleague Professor Giovanni Fantozzi? You will remember that he was transferred to Palermo from his chair in Naples. He finished the book after the move. It is a very fine work.'

'I am sure it is,' said von Igelfeld coldly. He had met Fantozzi and been unimpressed.

'Especially in respect of what it says about your own work,' Garelli-Ferrari went on.

Von Igelfeld frowned. 'It refers to . . . ' he began.

'To *Portuguese Irregular Verbs*,' said Garelli-Ferrari. 'He has an entire chapter on it. It's a sort of review article, I suppose – even if it's many years after your book's publication. I suppose some work doesn't date.'

'It does not,' said von Igelfeld firmly.

'He describes it as one of the great texts of European scholarship,' said Garelli-Ferrari. 'He puts it in the same class as Montaigne's *Essays* or Schopenhauer's *The World as Will and Representation*.'

Von Igelfeld hid his surprise behind a modest gesture. 'I would not presume to stand alongside such figures,' he said.

'Yet that is the company in which he puts you,' said Garelli-Ferrari. 'And I must say, I do not disagree.'

For a few moments von Igelfeld was lost for words. This extraordinary comparison, relayed to him through the unlikely agency of Professor Garelli-Ferrari, of all people, immediately cancelled the memory of the Italian scholar's paper. There was room for differences of opinion, and even if he could not really agree with the conclusions reached by Garelli-Ferrari in his paper, he had to admit that one could make a case for what he said, even if a woefully weak one.

Yet now von Igelfeld felt a sudden rush of affection for the

Italian scholar. To be compared to those towers of European thought was daunting, but encouraging nonetheless. 'You are most kind,' he said at last, smiling with the air of one conferring a benediction. 'Indeed, dear Professor Garelli-Ferrari, some would say that you are *too* kind.'

Garelli-Ferrari shook his head. 'I am only giving credit where it is due,' he said. 'I am merely repeating, with some pleasure, the opinions expressed by Fantozzi. He is a man of very sound judgement – as I suspect you have already heard.'

'But of course he is,' said von Igelfeld, adding hurriedly, 'Not in respect of what he says about me, of course. It is not for me to comment on that.' He paused. 'This book, though, the details have so far escaped me. When was it published?'

'It's yet to appear,' said Garelli-Ferrari. 'I believe it will be published in a couple of months. I received an advance copy from Fantozzi himself. He is my cousin, you see – a distant cousin, but we're related on my mother's side.'

This did not surprise von Igelfeld. He believed that most Italians were related to one another or, if they were not already so related, they eventually would be. 'I see,' he said. He did not wish to press too hard, but there was still much that he wished to find out.

He decided that nonchalance was appropriate. 'I expect I'll see it in due course,' he said. 'I shall get our librarian to order it – if he has not already done so. Herr Huber keeps a very close eye on all the new publications in the field. Very little escapes his attention.'

'You are very fortunate,' said Garelli-Ferrari. 'A good librarian is a great asset to any institution. Our own librarian has caused us some concern, I regret to say. He has been involved in certain illegal activities and is currently under investigation by the fiscal authorities.'

'That is most unfortunate,' said von Igelfeld. 'I hope that the matter is resolved before too long.'

Garelli-Ferrari sighed. 'These things take time. Our Rector's trial took years. Italian justice is not particularly quick.'

Von Igelfeld inclined his head in sympathy. 'Very upsetting.' He hesitated before continuing, 'And the publisher? Which publisher has Professor Fantozzi used?'

'It is a highly regarded academic publisher in Naples,' replied Garelli-Ferrari. 'They have a distinguished linguistic list. The publisher is also a cousin – a very distant one, though.'

Von Igelfeld waited for a few moments before venturing, 'Does dear Professor Fantozzi say much about me?' he asked.

'There are about fourteen full pages devoted to *Portuguese Irregular Verbs*,' replied Garelli-Ferrari. 'And a photograph.'

Von Igelfeld's heart skipped a beat. 'A photograph? A photograph of *Portuguese Irregular Verbs*?'

Garelli-Ferrari laughed. 'No, not of the book. A

photograph of yourself, Professor von Igelfeld. It's one taken when you received your honorary doctorate from the Gregorian University in Rome.'

Von Igelfeld waved a hand. 'Oh, that ... That was so long ago.'

'It's a very fine picture,' said Garelli-Ferrari.

Von Igelfeld said nothing, but he was now filled with goodwill towards Professor Garelli-Ferrari, Professor Fantozzi, and indeed towards the whole world of Italian scholarship. He smiled at the Italian, who returned the smile. 'You must read what he has to say,' he said to von Igelfeld. 'I expect you will be very pleased.'

Von Igelfeld nodded. He was thinking: how could he possibly wait two months to read this clearly very important Italian book? There must be ways of getting an advance copy. When he returned to Regensburg he would speak to Herr Huber and see how this could be arranged. He knew that Herr Huber would do whatever he could to help him, as he had always felt that the Librarian rather admired him. Dear Herr Huber, with his fussy ways and his interminable stories; with his modest ambitions and his low-key private life, led with that mousy wife of his in that small cottage in the woods outside town. Herr Huber would help him, and soon, with any luck, he would read what that generous, perspicacious Italian scholar had written. He would then send him a signed copy of *Portuguese Irregular Verbs*, as a thank-you. One good turn deserves another. We learned that as children, and von Igelfeld, who had been raised in the moral universe of the *Struwwelpeter*, was convinced that it was undeniably and perennially true.

Ex America semper aliquid novi

Like many academic institutions located in attractive cities, the Institute was regularly visited by scholars on sabbatical leave seeking congenial surroundings in which to pursue a scholarly project. Two visiting professors were shortly expected from Tulane University in New Orleans: Professor Pom Pom Boisseau, and her close companion and colleague, Professor Alice Martinique. The two Louisianians had some months ago proposed themselves for a five-week stay, and had now written to say that they would be arriving in Regensburg the following day. Their particular field of study was courtly poetry in various forms of Provençal, and they were currently working on the proofs of their jointly authored major work on the subject, to be published in Baton Rouge, Louisiana, later that year.

Their visit had been arranged a couple of months previously, but they had only just written to say when they would come and how they would travel. This was by motorcycle, as they had hired two red Ducatis from a garage in Munich and would arrive on those. When von Igelfeld broke the news that the visitors would be arriving the next day, he did so to a small audience in the Institute coffee room. Unterholzer had taken the morning off to visit his dentist, and so it was only Professor Prinzel and Herr Huber who were there to hear the news. Prinzel was particularly pleased by the impending visit and welcomed the prospect of discussions of the Occitan language. 'There are very few people working on the Provençal languages,' he said. 'This will complement our own work in many respects.'

Von Igelfeld gave him a sideways look. 'I would have thought that the French would have stepped up to the task,' he said. 'After all, the Provençal language is their province, or *Provence*, so to speak.'

Herr Huber smiled at the witticism. 'Very *drôle*, Professor von Igelfeld,' he said, adding, 'If I may be permitted to use a French loan-word.'

'Hah!' said von Igelfeld. '*Sehr witzig*, Herr Huber.' And then, becoming serious again, 'Occitan is indeed an interesting language. I have often thought of pursuing a bit of research into the version they speak down in Calabria. There's a small group of Occitan speakers near Cosenza, I believe.'

Herr Huber nodded. 'We have a rather strange monograph dealing with those people,' he said. 'I happened to notice it on the shelf the other day. It's called *The Language of the Lost Ultramontani*.'

Ex America semper aliquid novi

Von Igelfeld would normally have stopped listening at this point, as most people did when Herr Huber started one of his stories. Yet there was something about this that interested him.

'Why were these people lost?' he asked.

Herr Huber had a ready answer. 'They were not lost in the literal sense,' he said. They always knew where they were, I think.'

'I see,' said von Igelfeld.

'They were exiles from Piedmont,' Herr Huber continued. 'Religious persecution drove them down to the foot of Italy in the twelfth century. They were followers of a man called Peter Waldo, who took on the Catholic Church at the time. He was a banker who had trouble with his conscience. He gave everything away, including the interest he had charged people.' He paused. 'There are very few bankers like that these days, I'm afraid. I know the man who manages the bank near the pharmacy. You know the one? It has that large blue door. I can't see that man returning any interest – I really can't. I don't wish to do him an injustice, of course ...'

'No banker returns anything,' said Prinzel. 'It never happens.'

Von Igelfeld inclined his head. 'True,' he said.

'Life was something of a struggle for them, poor people,' Herr Huber continued. 'They call them Waldensians, you know. And they still exist – not in very large numbers, but you do find them – not only in Italy. There was a male nurse in my aunt's nursing home . . . '

'Yes, yes, Herr Huber,' said von Igelfeld, struggling to keep his voice from rising. Herr Huber, he had long believed, was a persistent moral challenge. 'We have heard all about that.'

Herr Huber took this interruption in his stride. 'They were excommunicated,' he said, 'and then driven away, taking their Occitan language with them. They had to endure centuries of discrimination. They still speak the language down there – a handful of them. It's mostly used around a town called Guardia Piemontese.' He paused. 'I have never been there, I'm afraid, although I did once pass through Cosenza and found that . . . '

Von Igelfeld made an impatient gesture. 'I know all about the Waldensians, Herr Huber,' he said. 'But I appreciate the history lesson nonetheless.'

Herr Huber seemed not to notice the reproach. 'There's more,' he said. 'I could find the book for you, if you wish.'

'Thank you,' said von Igelfeld. 'There is no time for such diversions at present.'

Herr Huber nodded. 'I am sure that these ladies from Louisiana will be able to tell us a great deal more about their particular form of Occitan. I have looked them up on the computer and have seen pictures of them at a conference in Missouri – on their motorbikes. They look very agreeable.'

Ex America semper aliquid novi

'I do not see the need for motorcycles,' said von Igelfeld. 'Trains provide perfectly adequate transport.'

Herr Huber thought for a moment. 'There are many people who enjoy the sensation of motorcycling. I have often thought of acquiring a motorcycle myself. Not a very large one, of course, but one that is capable of some speed, perhaps.'

Von Igelfeld gave the Librarian an incredulous look. 'You, Herr Huber? Would that be wise, do you think? One does not expect librarians ...' He cut himself short. Herr Huber was sensitive to remarks about librarians – unduly so, thought von Igelfeld.

'There is no reason why librarians should not ride motorcycles,' he said, in an injured tone.

'No, of course there isn't,' said von Igelfeld quickly. 'It's just that we expect librarians to be respectable, Herr Huber, and there is almost a presumption that people who ride motorcycles are ... unconventional, shall we say?'

Herr Huber considered this. 'I seem to recall something about this issue in the *American Libraries Magazine*,' he said. 'That is the monthly magazine for the American branch of the profession. They had a news item about a group of librarians who had formed a chapter of a motorcycle club. They wore leather jackets with a picture of a flying book on the back. There was a photograph of them.'

Von Igelfeld looked disapproving. 'One does not expect that sort of thing,' he said.

'I would not join a gang, of course,' said Herr Huber. 'You need have no fear of that, Professor von Igelfeld.'

'I should hope not, Herr Huber.' He decided to steer the conversation back to the visitors from Louisiana. 'I very much look forward to meeting these two ladies,' he said.

Prinzel had been listening to this exchange. Now he said, 'My wife has often said that it's about time we had some female colleagues. They will make for a refreshing change.'

Herr Huber looked thoughtful. 'We had Dr Schneeweiss,' he said. 'She was a woman. Remember her? And Dr Hilda Schreiber-Ziegler too.'

Von Igelfeld suppressed a shudder. 'They are not exactly regretted,' he said. 'But I hope that they are happy in their new positions. I trust that our new visitors will not be like them.'

Prinzel laughed. 'Bona fide visitors will never do what la Schreiber-Ziegler wanted to do – to take over the place.'

'Or laugh at people,' said Herr Huber. 'That was so ill-mannered of her.'

Von Igelfeld frowned. 'Did Dr Schreiber-Ziegler laugh at people?' he asked.

'Oh, yes,' said Herr Huber. 'She laughed a great deal at ... ' He stopped mid-sentence. He had been about to finish with 'at you'.

'Who did she laugh at?' asked von Igelfeld.

Herr Huber thought quickly. Unterholzer was not there.

To bring him into this was the safest way of dealing with the sudden awkwardness.

'I fear that she laughed at Professor Unterholzer,' he said. 'It was unforgivable.'

What he said was true: there had been an occasion on which Dr Schreiber-Ziegler had remarked that Unterholzer looked like a potato. That was a shocking thing to say, and he had never told anybody about it – and he did not propose to do so now.

But von Igelfeld was interested. Perhaps he was being too censorious about Dr Schreiber-Ziegler; Unterholzer was, in some respects, verging on the ridiculous. 'So, what did she say about our dear colleague?' he asked.

Herr Huber remained tight-lipped. 'I'm not sure I remember exactly,' he said.

Von Igelfeld was staring at him. 'I'm sure you do, Herr Huber. One does not forget these things that easily. If I saw somebody laughing at Professor Unterholzer, I am confident I would remember exactly what transpired – the *casus ioci*, one might say.'

Herr Huber's lower lip quivered. He had always been in awe of von Igelfeld, and he found himself unnerved by this probing. His voice lowered, he replied, 'She made an unflattering comparison.'

'To what?' pressed von Igelfeld.

Herr Huber swallowed hard. 'To a potato.'

Prinzel looked away, but von Igelfeld kept his gaze on

an embarrassed Herr Huber. Then he said, 'How very unfortunate.'

'Yes,' said Herr Huber. 'It was outrageous.'

'Although,' continued von Igelfeld, 'one might, perhaps, in the right light, that is, see a certain resemblance between our dear colleague and a potato. Not that it's a comparison that I would ever dream of invoking.'

'Of course not,' said Herr Huber.

'Although others might,' von Igelfeld added.

Herr Huber said nothing.

'Well at least we know that nobody could be as bad as Schneeweiss and Schreiber-Ziegler,' he said.

'*Ex America semper aliquid novi*,' remarked Prinzel.

Von Igelfeld gave Prinzel a severe look. 'In Pliny's time, Professor Prinzel, America did not exist.'

'But it did,' interjected Herr Huber. 'It was not *known* to exist, but that's not the same as not existing at all.'

Von Igelfeld sighed. 'That, Herr Huber,' he said, 'is neither here nor there.'

'The problem,' Prinzel now pronounced, 'is that we all think that the things that we, or those close to us, discover are being discovered for the first time. We all think that the world revolves around us. There are times when we could all do with a Nicolaus Copernicus to whisper in our ear.'

Von Igelfeld stared at him. He admired Prinzel, but there were times at which he could be distinctly unsettling. And von Igelfeld was sure that even if there were people who

Ex America semper aliquid novi

might benefit from a Copernican challenge, he himself was not one of them.

Herr Huber looked up. 'Copernicus never married,' he said. 'He was, however, very friendly with his housekeeper.'

This remark was greeted with silence. Eventually von Igelfeld said something. 'That may be, Herr Huber, but we should not allow ourselves to be distracted by tittle-tattle and scandal. Such things are not at all helpful.'

Herr Huber looked away, and von Igelfeld, feeling a pang of guilt, said in an emollient tone, 'Of course, that is very interesting, Herr Huber. The work of great men should always be considered in the light of what we know about their private lives.'

Prinzel said, 'Or women, of course. Did you know that the visions that Joan of Arc experienced were probably the result of an epileptic condition from which she suffered?'

'One of the patients in my aunt's nursing home,' said Herr Huber, 'a very charming former civil engineer from Würzburg originally – or was it Mainz? – I think it *might* have been Mainz – suffered from musico-genic seizures. He had to avoid listening to oompah bands. They were the main trigger.'

In the ensuing silence, nobody said anything until von Igelfeld eventually observed that the mid-morning pause – usually no more than thirty minutes – should come to an end, as they had been in the coffee room now for three-quarters of an hour. 'There is work to be done,' he said.

'That is always the case,' said Herr Huber, as he rose to his feet. 'There is work to be done – and yet it never seems to be *done* – in the sense of being completed.'

'Quite so,' said Prinzel. 'We may not work in a salt mine, but that does not mean there is no salt to be quarried.'

Herr Huber and von Igelfeld looked at Prinzel, uncertain as to how to interpret this comment. Eventually von Igelfeld said, 'We shall have to think about that, Professor Prinzel, although *prima facie* I would be inclined to agree.'

Herr Huber, taking his cue from von Igelfeld, nodded sagely. While von Igelfeld might give no further thought to what Prinzel had said, he certainly would.

A Mid-life Crisis?

It was Herr Huber who showed Pom Pom Boisseau and Alice Martinique to the office set aside for them. There were four rooms at the back of the Institute that had previously been used as storerooms and had been converted to provide office space for visitors and, occasionally, as overflow accommodation for the assistants – postgraduate students, for the most part, working as researchers for the academic staff. The American visitors had been allocated an office with two desks, a capacious bookcase, and an empty filing cabinet. From their window they had a view of hills across the roofs of the town.

'Perfection,' said Pom Pom, crossing the room to peer out of the window. 'I so miss the hills.'

Alice frowned. 'But, Pom Pom, we never had hills back home,' she pointed out.

Pom Pom shook a finger in mock reproach. 'That's why I

miss them,' she said. 'You miss things you never had more than the things you did have.'

Herr Huber smiled nervously. He had been confused by the name Pom Pom. Was it a contraction of something else – and if it was, would it be presumptuous of him to use the name?

Alice picked up his confusion. 'Pom Pom has always been called Pom Pom,' she said. 'That's the name we all have for her.'

Pom Pom agreed. 'I'd like you to use it, too,' she said. 'Officially, my name is Angel, but nobody ever calls me that. I've been Pom Pom since I was a little girl.'

Herr Huber made an effort. 'I shall do as you wish.' And then added, 'We try to make our guests feel at home.'

Pom Pom laughed. 'I wouldn't do that with us, honey,' she said. 'Have you ever been to New Orleans?'

'I'm afraid I have not,' said Herr Huber. 'I believe it's very ... '

'Different,' supplied Alice.

Herr Huber nodded. He had been taken aback by the informality of the visitors. He knew that Americans could be casual in their manner – their extraordinary habit of using first names, even with people they had known for no more than a few months, was surprising enough, but this use of the term *honey* went beyond even that. Was he expected to call them *honey* in return? He thought he probably was, as if he did not, it might seem standoffish to them – and he did not want that.

A Mid-life Crisis?

'I would like to visit New Orleans one day,' he said tentatively, before adding, 'honey.'

Pom Pom and Alice exchanged a glance. 'Well, that's just wonderful,' said Alice. 'We'd give you a good time, Hubie. Show you all the libraries, and so on.'

'Sure would,' agreed Pom Pom.

'Thank you, honey,' said Herr Huber.

Pom Pom now asked him about the staff of the Institute. 'There's you, of course,' she said, 'and there's Professor von Igelfeld. We've exchanged a lot of messages, he and I. We sure look forward to meeting him.'

'It's always interesting meeting people in the flesh after you've had dealings with them by mail,' said Alice.

'That is very true,' said Herr Huber. 'I often imagine people incorrectly, and then am surprised when I see them.'

Alice smiled at him encouragingly. 'And how did you imagine us, Herr Huber? Are we what you expected?'

Herr Huber blushed. 'Oh, I'm not sure that I thought about that.'

Pom Pom exchanged a glance with Alice. Then, in a teasing tone, she said, 'You must have had some idea.'

Herr Huber looked away. 'I was intrigued to hear that you would arrive by motorcycle. That interested me.'

Pom Pom raised an eyebrow. 'Interested you? Why was that?'

Herr Huber showed his confusion. 'Oh, I don't know

why. You don't really think of professors as riding motorcycles. Or ladies, for that matter. Many ladies think that motorcycles are a bit too ... '

They waited for him to finish, but he trailed away.

'A bit too what?' asked Pom Pom.

'Oh, I don't know,' said Herr Huber. 'I'm not sure that I meant to say that. It's just that motorcycles are a bit *masculine* ... '

Pom Pom pretended to be surprised. 'Oh, I've never heard that,' she said. Then, turning to Alice, she said, 'Have you heard that motorcycles are considered masculine, honey?'

Alice shook her head. 'Never heard that,' she said.

Herr Huber was now thoroughly embarrassed. He had been discreetly looking at the two visitors and had noticed fairly substantial muscles underneath their full-sleeved shirts. And Pom Pom, he thought, had a very strong chin when looked at from a certain angle. Of course, women these days were participating in all sorts of sports that used to be the preserve of men – boxing and wrestling, and so on, were all open to women and encouraged muscular development. Perhaps you had to be strong to ride one of those big motorcycles.

He decided to change the subject. 'I expect that you would like some time to settle in,' he said. 'I would be delighted to give you a tour of our library facilities, but perhaps we can do that tomorrow, when we can do it in a more leisurely way.'

'That would be just great,' said Pom Pom.

'Yes, fine,' agreed Alice.

'And don't hesitate to call me if you need anything,' said Herr Huber.

'We shall,' said Pom Pom, pointing a playful finger at him. 'We'll come straight to you, honey.'

'Well, I'll leave you to settle in,' said Herr Huber, adding, slightly lamely, 'honeys.'

He left, and once he had gone, Pom Pom turned to Alice and said, 'Pretty cute, don't you think.'

'In a teddy-bear-ish sort of way,' said Alice.

Pom Pom looked at her watch. 'I could murder a drink,' she said.

'Me too,' said Alice. 'Let's go to that bar we saw mentioned in the guide.'

'Great idea.'

They made their way downstairs and out of the building. Once they were astride their motorcycles, they switched on the engines and revved sharply. A small flock of ravens, disturbed by the shattering sound of the Ducatis, flew up from a tree in which they had been sheltering. They climbed into the air, cawing and protesting at the uproar below.

Professor Dr Unterholzer made his way purposefully along the corridor that led to von Igelfeld's office. His own room was at the opposite end of the building, although he would very much have preferred to be closer to the library and the coffee room, as were the rooms occupied by von Igelfeld and Prinzel. It was typical of von Igelfeld, Unterholzer thought, that he should have so engineered things that he got the office that not only had the best view, but that was coolest in summer and warmest in winter. Unterholzer was convinced that von Igelfeld had somehow used his influence with the Rector to secure favourable treatment – his own requests for alterations to his room had met with a stony, almost derisory response from the Works Department. The director of that particular department, Unterholzer had noticed, had by far the finest office in the University – considerably better than the Rector's – and even the director's secretary occupied an office with an anteroom, a private washroom, and a small kitchenette in which to prepare lunch.

But now was not the time to rehearse these well-founded grudges; Unterholzer had more urgent business than that to discuss with von Igelfeld. In particular, he wanted to seek an explanation of what he had just seen through his inadequate and ill-placed window.

'My dear Professor Unterholzer,' von Igelfeld said, looking up from his desk. 'This is an unexpected pleasure.'

Unterholzer made a non-committal response. Then he said, 'I take it I'm not interrupting anything important.'

He said this in such a way as to suggest that it was highly

unlikely that von Igelfeld had anything important to do, and that was how von Igelfeld interpreted the remark.

Von Igelfeld, of course, was scrupulously polite to Unterholzer. 'Oh, nothing too vital, Professor Unterholzer,' came his reply. 'I have just returned from a conference in Berlin – as you probably know.'

Unterholzer made an airy gesture, as if to suggest that von Igelfeld's conference was of no importance to him.

Von Igelfeld noticed this. He suspected that Unterholzer had not been invited and was feeling resentful as a result. In normal circumstances, von Igelfeld would have tactfully refrained from mentioning the conference, but Unterholzer's apparent judgement on its unimportance rankled. The implication was inescapable: von Igelfeld, Unterholzer thought, had nothing better to do than attend inconsequential conferences in Berlin.

'It was a fascinating meeting,' von Igelfeld said. 'I was half expecting to see you there, but I didn't. I think you would have enjoyed it, Professor Unterholzer.'

Unterholzer's lip curled. 'I have been very busy,' he said. 'I do not have time to attend every meeting that takes place here, there and everywhere.' He paused. 'And that ridiculous Professor Garelli-Ferrari – I assume you had to put up with his waffling on about Neanderthal vowel sounds.'

Von Igelfeld caught his breath. Professor Garelli-Ferrari had explicitly said that he had shown his paper to

Unterholzer – and the reaction had been enthusiastic. This was duplicity on a world-class scale. He waited for a moment before he made the observation that would, he imagined, give Unterholzer cause to think. He spoke now with measured precision. 'But I believe you read the paper before he delivered it. He said you approved.'

Unterholzer made a strange choking sound – as well he might, thought von Igelfeld. 'I . . . I . . . ' he stuttered.

Von Igelfeld had no desire to further embarrass Unterholzer. It was hard enough *being* Unterholzer, without additional humiliations being thrown in. So now, in a conciliatory tone, he said, 'No matter. Neanderthal linguistics are a matter of complete speculation. I really don't think any rational person need concern himself with them.'

Unterholzer made a sound that might have been an indication of agreement or just a clearing of the throat. Whatever it was, von Igelfeld felt that he had made his point, and so he enquired of Unterholzer what brought him to his office.

'I have just seen the most extraordinary sight,' said Unterholzer. 'I happened to be looking out of my window, and I saw two ladies mounting large motorcycles parked in the Institute car park. They were wearing leather jackets – and leather trousers. They made a dreadful noise and then shot off.'

Von Igelfeld smiled. 'Those were our visitors, Professor Unterholzer.'

A Mid-life Crisis?

Had von Igelfeld announced the Second Coming, Unterholzer could not have been more surprised. He opened his mouth to speak, but no sound came. Then, a full minute later, he managed, 'They are the two American professors?'

'Yes,' said von Igelfeld. 'Professor Pom Pom Boisseau and Professor Alice Martinique. Both are from New Orleans, as you probably know from the note I sent out some weeks ago.'

'But the motorcycles . . .' Unterholzer spluttered.

'They are keen motorcyclists, I believe,' said von Igelfeld. 'They have hired those machines for use while they are with us here in Regensburg.'

Unterholzer struggled to make sense of an incomprehensible situation. 'What will people say?' he asked.

Von Igelfeld shrugged. 'I don't think they will say anything very much. I suspect that people will barely remark on the situation.'

Unterholzer shook his head. 'I never imagined it would come to this.' He paused. 'Have they been installed yet?'

'I asked Herr Huber to show them to their room,' replied von Igelfeld.

'Herr Huber!' expostulated Unterholzer. 'Do you think he'll be able to cope?'

Von Igelfeld tried to calm the situation. 'Herr Huber is more worldly than you imagine,' he said. 'And I suspect that he will have formed a very favourable impression of them. I only met them briefly, but they seemed quite charming.'

Unterholzer seemed once again to be lost for words. Eventually, though, he ordered his thoughts sufficiently to say, 'I shudder to think how people will react if they see people like that – bikers, they call them – admitted to the very heart of our Institute. Can you imagine how shocked they will be? Our reputation, Professor von Igelfeld, is about to be irretrievably ruined.' He fixed von Igelfeld with a rueful stare. 'We shall be a complete laughing stock throughout the country.'

For a moment or two von Igelfeld did not react. Then he raised an eyebrow – a tactic he had often used – successfully, in most instances – when responding to something that Unterholzer had said. 'Oh, come now, Professor Dr Unterholzer,' he began. 'Surely you overstate the problem slightly. Are you really suggesting that dogs will bark at us in the street? That small boys will run behind us, throwing stones and shouting insults about the company we're keeping? Will anybody even notice Pom Pom and Alice?'

Unterholzer's jaw dropped. This was almost too much to take in. That von Igelfeld, of all people, should suddenly start referring to these two visitors as 'Pom Pom and Alice' would, until a few seconds ago, have seemed inconceivable, and yet he had now heard it himself, in circumstances where there was no possibility that he had misunderstood what was being said. He stared at von Igelfeld, and then blinked. Could it be that von Igelfeld

A Mid-life Crisis?

had suddenly lost his reason? Unterholzer had read that psychotic episodes can be sudden and unannounced – that one moment one is behaving rationally and in character, and the next one might spout inexplicable nonsense. It was all to do with brain chemistry, he believed. Things went wrong with the chemicals that enabled brain cells to communicate, and before you knew it you were in the grip of florid delusions.

Unterholzer's wife, Frau Professor Dr Unterholzer, had a cousin, Klaus-Peter, who was a psychiatrist and who had spoken of a case where a man woke up in the morning and asked his wife why they appeared to be at the Munich Beer Festival. They were not, of course – they were in their flat in Frankfurt, but he was convinced that there were waiters outside the door with large steins of beer and that a brass band was playing in the bathroom. Prior to that morning, the poor man was an entirely rational physics teacher at a technical high school. The descent into delusional thinking had been profound, and had lasted for several days before his thoughts once again became ordered. Had something similar happened to von Igelfeld?

Unterholzer was cautious. 'May I ask, Professor von Igelfeld, whether you are feeling quite right? The sun has been rather hot of late, and it's possible that ...'

Von Igelfeld made a dismissive gesture. 'If you are asking me whether I'm confused,' he said, 'then the answer is an unequivocal no. I have not had too much sun. Nor have I had too much of anything else – if you are suspicious about that.'

Unterholzer shook his head, as if trying to come to terms with the implications of von Igelfeld's unexpected insouciance. 'I suppose you think I'm old-fashioned,' he said. 'I suppose you think I'm putting far too much stress on things that don't count for very much any longer. I suppose you think I belong in the past ...'

This was powerful rhetoric, and von Igelfeld looked momentarily taken aback by Unterholzer's outburst. But then he smiled. 'We must all move with the times, Professor Unterholzer. It will be given to some of us to be in the vanguard, while others may perhaps find it a little more difficult to adjust. But we must all try.'

Unterholzer stood quite still as he absorbed the implications of what had just been said. The world might still be spinning on its accustomed axis, but somewhere deep in its fundament, something had changed. If von Igelfeld was becoming indifferent to the reputation of the Institute of Romance Philology, then what hope was there of maintaining the Academy's defences against the tides of vulgarisation lapping at its shores? Very little, he thought – or perhaps even none.

Then a deeply unsettling idea occurred to him. Once again, he thought about his wife's cousin Klaus-Peter. He had said something about mid-life crises the other day – about how common, almost universal, they were – and about how they could, for a short period, turn everything upside down. It had never occurred to Unterholzer that von Igelfeld would ever undergo anything quite so ordinary as a mid-life crisis, but he was only human, like the rest of men, and could not be expected to be immune to the embarrassments to which the flesh was heir. Yes, thought Unterholzer: this was an entirely feasible explanation. And if it were to be the *fons et origo* of von Igelfeld's odd behaviour, then at least it was possible that something could be done. He would speak to Cousin Klaus-Peter and ask him for advice. More than that: he would sound his wife out about the possibility of hosting a dinner party to which both von Igelfeld and Klaus-Peter would be invited. That would provide an opportunity for his colleague to be assessed by a psychiatrist – discreetly, of course – and action to be taken. And then Unterholzer had a further, and completely tantalising idea: if von Igelfeld could be declared to be insane, then the University would have no alternative but to suspend him during the period of his treatment – or preferably indefinitely – and that would mean that Unterholzer would be able to get his room. There was no point in leaving a room locked up and empty while its occupant was receiving residential psychiatric treatment, and this was particularly the case when the room in question was one of the most desirable of all university offices. He, Unterholzer, would be ready to move in, and would be only too happy to help put von Igelfeld's books in storage in the basement, or even throw a number of them out. There was no need, Unterholzer thought, to have twenty-eight copies of *Portuguese Irregular Verbs* cluttering up the bookshelves; twenty-seven of these could be passed on to one of those firms that pulped old books. That would be in the spirit of ecological awareness that the University seemed so intent on fostering in its staff. Well, Unterholzer would oblige – with pleasure.

In the meantime, though, he would have to handle von Igelfeld with considerable caution. Lunatics could be very strong, Unterholzer knew: some said they had the strength of three men. Unterholzer realised that he should not say anything that might tip von Igelfeld further into the embrace of unreason. And so he changed the subject, saying nothing further about the American visitors, and raising, instead, an obscure editorial point connected with a future edition of the *Zeitschrift*.

Von Igelfeld gave a perfectly coherent reply, which only went to show, Unterholzer thought, how cunning mentally disordered people could be. He would have to speak to Prinzel and warn him of the danger. Prinzel was level-headed and also physically strong. That could be useful if the worst came to the worst and von Igelfeld became violent. Prinzel would be able to restrain him, Unterholzer thought, at least until help arrived and von Igelfeld could be taken off in an ambulance to somewhere where he might be sedated and kept out of harm's way.

A Mid-life Crisis?

Unterholzer shook his head. It was sad that things should end this way, but at least von Igelfeld could be given treatment, and his dignity be protected. That was something for which one might feel grateful.

A Motorcycle Fantasy

The following day, von Igelfeld sought out Herr Huber in the office he occupied at the back of the Institute's library. The wording of the notice on Herr Huber's door had always irritated von Igelfeld, and now it did so doubly. *Library Director*, it proclaimed; *Consultations by appointment unless otherwise arranged.* The title of *Library Director*, von Igelfeld thought, had never been approved by the University authorities. Herr Huber was a librarian *simpliciter* – he was not a director of anything. If anybody were to be allowed to call themselves directors, then where would it all end? Frau Schlaginhauffen, who ran the Institute canteen, and whose *Münchner Weisswurst* was so widely appreciated, might start styling herself *Wurstdirektor*, or something equally ridiculous – in fact, anybody at all could be some sort of director if this sort of thing were to go unchecked. And as for this business of appointments – since when, von Igelfeld asked himself, did one need an appointment to talk to a librarian?

Librarians should consider themselves fortunate if professors took the time to talk to them; they were certainly not important enough to require an appointment.

Of course, if anybody were to get an appointment to speak to Herr Huber, they would be very likely to regret it. They would discover just how difficult it was to get a word in edgeways once Herr Huber launched himself on any particular subject. And they would discover, too, just how hard it was to steer any conversation with Herr Huber back to the matter in hand. There would be far too much to say about Italian state railways, about the quirks of academic publishers, about nursing homes and the staff that ran them – about anything, in fact, other than the literature on Romance philology, which is what Herr Huber should be prepared to talk about.

Von Igelfeld put these thoughts out of his mind as he knocked on Herr Huber's door. From within came the Librarian's faint *herein*.

'I do not have an appointment,' von Igelfeld began. 'I trust that you will forgive my imposing myself like this, Herr Huber.'

Herr Huber, who had been sat at his desk, sprang to his feet. 'But Professor von Igelfeld, if there is anybody who is entitled to impose – not that I'm saying that you *are* imposing – then it surely must be you.'

'How very kind,' said von Igelfeld. 'I shall not take up much of your time.'

Herr Huber pointed to the chair on the other side of his desk. 'I would be obliged if you sat down,' he said. 'There is a chair.'

'So I see,' said von Igelfeld.

Von Igelfeld lowered himself onto the seat of the straight-backed chair indicated by Herr Huber. 'You must be very busy,' he said. 'I've always been astonished at how much work you librarians get through . . . All that cataloguing . . .'

'Library directors,' Herr Huber corrected. 'Yes, we are at times extremely busy – and not just with cataloguing – although that is central to our endeavours. We need more people to do all the tasks expected of us. We need more junior directors prepared to give up what one has to give up in order to follow a calling in librarianship. It is not quite a vow of chastity, Professor von Igelfeld, but I have always thought it is not all that much different. Librarianship is a vocation, much the same as is monasticism.'

Von Igelfeld nodded. This was such nonsense, but he had come to ask a favour of Herr Huber and it cost him nothing to agree with him on these unimportant matters.

'I very much hope,' Herr Huber continued, 'that one of these days the University will increase library budgets and enable us to appoint more library staff. But do they see the need? I'm afraid they don't.' He thought of Herr Uber-Huber, from the University administration, who had been so overbearing in his dealings with the Institute. The sheer effrontery of that man . . .

Von Igelfeld inclined his head sympathetically. 'Of course, Herr Huber, it is possible that I might be able to help any approach you make to the powers that be. I am not without influence in administrative circles, I believe. Not that I would want to abuse my position ...'

'Of course not,' said Herr Huber quickly. 'But at the same time, if you were able to have a discreet word with His Magnificence, the Rector, I can't imagine that it would do any harm.'

'All my words are discreet,' said von Igelfeld.

Herr Huber laughed nervously. 'Oh, that is very amusing indeed, Professor von Igelfeld. I hope that I shall be permitted to record that in my diary – such a witty remark.'

'Please do,' said von Igelfeld. 'And I shall try later on to say something equally witty – so that you have a choice when you are talking more widely about the nature of academic humour. You may even want to quote both yourself and me in the same report. Our words could complement one another, I imagine.'

Herr Huber seemed pleased. 'Oh, that is such a positive thing to say. In a world that is devoid, it sometimes seems, of joy and optimism, comes an aperçu that is both benevolent and profoundly true. How fortunate I am to be the beneficiary of such wisdom.'

Von Igelfeld looked pained. 'Please, Herr Huber, do not put Pelion upon Ossa. Suffice it to say that our collaboration is getting off to an excellent start.' He paused. 'Which

A Motorcycle Fantasy

reminds me: I wanted to ask your professional opinion, Herr Huber. I need your advice about a book.'

Herr Huber looked up from his desk. 'But that is exactly what I am for,' he said. 'It is my *raison d'être* to provide such advice – with or without an appointment.'

It was von Igelfeld's turn to note the witticism. 'Very funny, Herr Huber. *Très amusant*, as our dear French colleagues might say – if they ever saw anything as funny, that is . . .'

'Hah!' said Herr Huber. 'You know how they say the French have no sense of humour. You have their measure, Professor von Igelfeld – there can be no doubt about that.'

Herr Huber sat back in his chair, clearly enjoying this warm and informal exchange. But von Igelfeld had asked about a book, and he must respond to that. 'Please tell me,' he said, 'what book you are interested in, Professor von Igelfeld. I pride myself on being able to find virtually anything – just like the Canadian Mounties. They were always said to get their man, I believe. You may have seen that old film *Rose Marie*, with Nelson Eddy and Jeanette MacDonald. Nelson Eddy was the Mountie – he had a very fine singing voice. My aunt always admired him, although fewer and fewer people remember him these days. Or Richard Tauber, for that matter. He was a very great Austrian lyric tenor, as I'm sure you will recall, Professor von Igelfeld. He was in *The Student Prince*.'

Von Igelfeld listened politely. The important thing was to

The Lost Language of Oysters

wait for Herr Huber to draw breath, and to make a quick interjection then. That opportunity now arose.

'Yes, yes, Herr Huber,' said von Igelfeld. 'We must not forget Richard Tauber. But I was wondering about a book that I believe is just about to be published. It was mentioned to me by Professor Garelli-Ferrari when I met him recently at a conference in Berlin.'

Herr Huber frowned. This, von Igelfeld realised, was a bad sign, as it signalled the appearance of yet another rabbit-hole. Von Igelfeld was about to make a remark that would bring them back to the matter he had come to discuss, but it was too late.

'Garelli-Ferrari?' asked Herr Huber. 'That is a very unusual name. He must be a member of the rather distinguished Garelli-Ferraris who still inhabit the Palazzo Garelli-Ferrari in the Trastevere. They are one of those old Roman families known as the *nobiltà nera*. The old Roman titles were conferred by the popes. They were the ones who carried the Pope's chair – in the days when popes were borne around St Peter's shoulder-high. It was a dangerous way to get about – it would not do if one of the nobles carrying you stumbled.' He paused. 'I read recently of another fine noble Italian family, as it happens. There is a family called Bianco di San Secondo Biondi. They have a very unusual name, of course, but it would be very difficult for a librarian to know where to file a book by such a person ... '

'Indeed,' said von Igelfeld quickly. 'But this is not really

A Motorcycle Fantasy

about Professor Garelli-Ferrari. He mentioned a book by a colleague of his, one Professor Fantozzi. It is not yet published, I believe, or, if it has been published, it has only very recently been made available.'

Herr Huber stroked his chin. 'Now, let me think,' he said. 'Fantozzi, Fantozzi, Fantozzi . . . Yes, indeed: Fantozzi.'

Von Igelfeld waited. After a moment or two of silence, Herr Huber continued, 'We have that book, as it happens. I remember now. We received a special advance copy. The book itself will not be published for another month, I believe, but our supplier sent a surplus review copy. I think that must be the book you are asking about.'

Von Igelfeld felt a surge of excitement. Now he would be able to sit down and read the entire chapter devoted to *Portuguese Irregular Verbs*. Now he would be able to savour the unstinting praise of the generous-spirited Professor Fantozzi.

'I would like to consult it,' he said to Herr Huber. 'Could you possibly locate it for me?'

Herr Huber nodded. 'I can certainly do that,' he said. 'If you would care to wait for a moment, I shall go off and fetch it. I think it will be in the cataloguing room. Young Herr Hühnerbein will be preparing the index entries for it and a lot of other new books we have recently received. He is very efficient, that young man. Do you know that his mother . . . '

'Thank you, Herr Huber,' said von Igelfeld, rather too sharply.

The Lost Language of Oysters

'... was a professional wrestler,' Herr Huber trailed off.

The Librarian now rose from his chair and left the room. Von Igelfeld smiled to himself. Poor Herr Huber: he lived in a world full of superfluous and irrelevant facts – professional wrestling, Italian nobility, blood-pressure pills – and yet he was always keen to help in any way he could. It could be frustrating trying to keep him to the point, but he rarely said anything unkind about others. He was at heart a good man, if a rather fussy one.

It did not take Herr Huber long. Five minutes later he returned to his office. Von Igelfeld noticed that he was empty-handed.

'I'm very sorry,' Herr Huber began. 'I was hoping to be able to give you the book, but unfortunately that is not possible.'

Von Igelfeld could not conceal his disappointment. 'Your Herr Hühnerbein is still working on it?'

Herr Huber shook his head. 'No, he has finished cataloguing it.'

Von Igelfeld waited.

Herr Huber gave him an apologetic look. 'The book was placed in the shelves, apparently – and has been borrowed by a reader.'

Von Igelfeld sighed. 'I'm sorry to hear that.' He paused. 'Which reader? One of the assistants?'

Herr Huber looked embarrassed. 'I'm afraid I can't tell you that,' he said. 'I'd like to, but I can't.'

Von Igelfeld gave him an impatient look. 'You don't have

a record of who takes books out of the library? Surely that can't be possible, Herr Huber.'

Herr Huber was indignant. 'Of course we keep a record, Professor von Igelfeld. That is a fundamental duty of a librarian – to know where the books are.'

'Well then,' said von Igelfeld. 'You must know who the reader is. Unless, of course, the reader in question came into the library heavily disguised. That is always possible, I suppose.'

Herr Huber seemed to miss the irony. 'The reason I can't tell you,' he said, 'is that the borrowing data of the library are confidential.'

'Confidential?' exploded von Igelfeld. 'May I remind you, Herr Huber, that I am a member of the Governing Committee of the Institute.' He might have added that he was the author of *Portuguese Irregular Verbs*, holder of three doctorates, two of which were honorary, and the recipient of the German Government's *Großes Verdienstkreuz mit Stern und Schulterband*, awarded for services to Romance linguistic scholarship. All of that might have been added, but he did not feel that it should be necessary for somebody in his position to explain to a librarian why the petty rules of a library should not be applied to him.

Herr Huber looked down at his feet. He was clearly miserable. 'These are the rules,' he began. 'I did not draw up the rules, Professor von Igelfeld. I would not like you to think that I drew up such restrictive regulations.'

'I would never accuse you of such pettiness,' said von Igelfeld in an emollient tone. 'And I assure you that if you interpret the rules constructively in my case, I shall not reveal to anybody that you have been able to see beyond these ridiculous restrictions.'

For a few moments it seemed as if Herr Huber might break into tears. Sensing this, von Igelfeld said, 'This is not your decision, Herr Huber. I take full responsibility.'

This was the let-out that Herr Huber had been hoping for. 'In that case, Professor von Igelfeld, I can reveal to you that the reader who borrowed the book was our esteemed colleague, Professor Dr Unterholzer.'

Von Igelfeld received this information passively. 'In that case,' he said. 'Could you please recall the book? Tell Professor Unterholzer that it is needed by another reader.'

'But I can't do that,' protested Herr Huber. 'The rules say that readers are entitled to keep a book out on loan for a maximum period of six weeks. Apparently, Professor Dr Unterholzer borrowed it only yesterday.'

'But if you took a constructive view of the confidentiality rule,' said von Igelfeld, 'then surely you can do the same with this ridiculous six-week rule.'

Herr Huber shook his head. He was not enjoying this. 'I cannot do anything about that category of rule. The confidentiality rule is an Institute rule – this other rule is a rule of the University. That is unassailable, I very much regret to say. That rule draws its authority from the State

Parliament and has the full backing of law. I am very sorry about that, Professor von Igelfeld, but we are, as you well know, a *Rechtsstaat*. We cannot simply ignore those laws we do not like.'

Von Igelfeld bit his lip. This was intolerable. He would have to speak to Unterholzer about this; he would have to appeal to his better nature – if indeed there was a better nature under that rather lumpy exterior. But before he did that, he tried one more approach to Herr Huber.

'Do you think you might be able to obtain a further copy from the publisher?' he asked.

Herr Huber shook his head again. 'I'm afraid it was an advance copy. They said in their letter that no further copies were available. I fear that we shall have to wait, Professor von Igelfeld.'

Von Igelfeld rose to leave. He thanked Herr Huber for his help, somehow concealing his irritation. It was not poor Herr Huber's fault – he was a minor cog in a large machine and had done everything he could. No, it was Unterholzer who was to blame here. There could be no doubt but that Unterholzer had heard of the chapter it contained on *Portuguese Irregular Verbs* and was deliberately preventing von Igelfeld from reading it. It was exceptionally petty, but then what could one expect of Unterholzer, who had so little to do with his time? It was a phenomenon that von Igelfeld had noticed before: those with the least to do tended to be at the same time those who made the most of unimportant matters. It was a universal feature of human nature, he supposed, but it rankled nonetheless. And behind it all, he decided, there lurked an unmentionable matter: background. Unterholzer came from an obscure potato-growing district. The people there were worthy in their way, but they were not noted for their broad outlook and culture. Their main interests were potatoes, beer festivals and traditional dancing in which the men in their lederhosen slapped their thighs and kicked one another in the seat of the pants. That explained Unterholzer; that was his cultural hinterland. And yet he reminded himself that he should try to be generous towards his colleague, whatever his failings were. We all had our faults, and even if Unterholzer's were both manifold and egregious, he was still an old friend and should be treated with tolerance and compassion. Unterholzer had so little in his life compared with what I have, thought von Igelfeld. His book on the subjunctive ... well, the least said about that, the better. Poor Frau Unterholzer was so unprepossessing, even in a good light; and then there was that unfortunate dog of theirs, the dachshund that had lost its legs in that regrettable accident – a veterinary student's fault, over which a veil had to be drawn – and was now reliant on a strapped-on undercarriage with three wheels. Von Igelfeld imagined them going for a walk, the three of them: Unterholzer, Frau Unterholzer and Walter, the dog. It was a strangely poignant picture, and he put it out of his mind with a sad shake of the head. There were so many little tragedies in this life, and there was a limit to how much one should contemplate them.

But now Herr Huber made a final suggestion. 'You could always go to the local authorities, I suppose. You could ask them to amend the law by administrative fiat. That can be done with low-level regulations.'

Von Igelfeld looked thoughtful. 'Should I approach a politician?' he asked.

Herr Huber nodded. 'There is one particular politician in this area who has the reputation of being very helpful. He is a certain Herr Andreas Durchdenwald. They call him Durchi in the newspapers.'

'And where would I find this *sogennant* Durchi?' asked von Igelfeld.

'I pass his house every day on my way in to the Institute,' said Herr Huber. 'I shall write the address down on this piece of paper.'

Von Igelfeld took the proffered slip of paper, thanked Herr Huber once again, and made his way out into the library.

'Why, it's you, Moritz-Maria,' came a loud whisper from behind a book stack.

He spun round. It was Professor Pom Pom Boisseau. She was dressed in tight-fitting blue jeans and an army camouflage shirt. She wore a pair of heavy hiking boots.

Von Igelfeld was surprised to see her, but, at the same time, pleased. She is a truly splendid woman, he thought. She was exceptional. So *masterful*. So full of *promise*.

'This is a great pleasure,' he said. 'I hope that you are finding everything you need to find in the library.'

Pom Pom laughed. 'Enough to keep going with,' she said. 'And you never know what you're going to find after that, do you?'

Von Igelfeld smiled. There was something about the way she talked that appealed to him. And there was another quality, too, that he could not help noticing – a pulsing energy, perhaps. It was very powerful.

'Would you care to join me for a cup of tea at the end of the working day?' he asked.

The invitation came out before he had time to think of it.

'Do dogs bark?' replied Pom Pom.

Von Igelfeld was taken aback. What had dogs to do with this?

'They certainly do bark,' he said.

This brought a peal of laughter from Pom Pom. 'Oh, you're a scream!' she said. Her voice was plummy. It was, von Igelfeld thought, the sort of voice that a large *Stollen* cake would have, could such cakes talk. It was a voice rich in marzipan and orange zest.

They agreed the time at which they would meet, and von Igelfeld made his way back to his office. He felt strangely light-headed – even excited. And once back in his office he found it surprisingly difficult to concentrate on his work. He remembered Pom Pom's jeans, and the boots. He remembered her rather appealing smile, and the redness of her lips.

A Motorcycle Fantasy

He smiled to himself – a warm, *interested* smile. She was not very feminine, he felt, but did that matter? He thought it did not, and then, after that thought, came another one. Could he be falling in love with Professor Pom Pom Boisseau? Surely not. Von Igelfeld had never thought very much about romance – there had always been so many other things to do, such as writing *Portuguese Irregular Verbs* and running the Institute. But it was always possible, he thought, that one day he would meet somebody with whom he might get on rather well. Was this what was happening? Was Professor Pom Pom Boisseau of Tulane University, New Orleans, Louisiana, that person? He closed his eyes and allowed his mind to wander. He pictured Pom Pom on her motorbike, the wind streaming through her hair. He saw himself riding pillion behind her, his arms around her waist. And the sound of the Ducati, the roaring, and the countryside unfolding as they shot down the road. He opened his eyes. Should he even be *thinking* this sort of thing?

Cauliflower Cheese

Professor Pom Pom Boisseau was fifteen minutes late in coming to von Igelfeld's room that evening. She made no excuse, but breezed in through the open door and tossed her bag down on the floor before saying brightly, as if nothing had happened, 'So, what's new, Moritz-Maria?'

Von Igelfeld struggled to compose himself. He could not help but look at his watch, pointedly enough for his visitor to notice. But this did not elicit any explanation for Pom Pom's tardiness, and so he answered her question with a witticism. 'What's new? Shall I say, *Ex mihi nunquam aliquid novi.*' It was a brilliant play on Pliny's famous statement; the response that there was never anything new from him was self-effacing as much as it was a jest.

At first, Pom Pom gave him a blank look, but then her face broke into a broad smile. 'So we're in for a *Plinary* session.'

Von Igelfeld was impassive. 'Not necessarily,' he said. And then continued, 'I was concerned that you might have forgotten our arrangement. I am very relieved, though, that you are here.'

Pom Pom looked surprised. 'Forget? No, not me. I never forget things. Did you forget?'

Von Igelfeld shook his head. 'No, I thought you might have forgotten. It's six-fifteen, you see, and I thought ...'

She cut him short. 'Oh, my, I had forgotten. Not forgotten that we were meeting, of course, but how keen you people are on doing things on the dot. Sorry about that. Where I come from, back in Louisiana, we take a more relaxed view of time. Six o'clock means some time before eight, mostly.'

Von Igelfeld drew in his breath. How was it possible to take a relaxed view of time? Time moved at the same pace whether one was in New Orleans or Regensburg, or wherever. He felt a surge of irritation, but this dissipated quickly. He was relieved that she was here – that was the important thing.

'It doesn't matter,' he said. 'What's the difference between six and six-fifteen in the overall scale of things?'

'Fifteen minutes?' said Pom Pom, and laughed.

'Hah!' exclaimed von Igelfeld. 'That's very amusing, Professor ...'

She raised a finger. 'None of that. None of that Professor Dr stuff. I'm Pom Pom, pure and simple. Even my students back home call me that.'

Von Igelfeld gasped. 'Your students? You let your students call you by ... by your first name? Is that wise.'

Pom Pom shrugged. 'It's my name. I see no reason why they can't use it.' She paused. 'Of course, some of the young men call me ma'am. It's that old-fashioned thing they have down in the South, you see. These guys still wear ties, some of them.'

Von Igelfeld frowned. He wore a tie. Was there something wrong with that?

Pom Pom now sat down, uninvited. 'Nice chair,' she said.

Von Igelfeld nodded. 'I am very fortunate to have this office,' he said, looking about him. 'My colleagues would rather like to have it, I suspect.'

Pom Pom laughed. 'Oh, that's a standard thing in universities. It's the one big thing, in fact. Who has what office – it probably causes more trouble than anything else. Forget disagreements over scholarly questions – think offices. That way, you'll understand what goes on in a university.'

'Is it the same at your institution?' asked von Igelfeld.

'Completely. Alice and I both have great offices, and there's this guy who really resents that fact. He's got a perfectly good office, but he thinks that he should have somewhere better. He says we only got ours because we were friendly with the Dean, who's Harley-Davidson. That's what we ride.'

Von Igelfeld looked confused. He was not sure whether he should know of this Professor Harley-Davidson. 'Harley-Davidson?' he asked.

Pom Pom stared at him, as if uncertain how to take his

question. Then she smiled. 'That's the name of a bike. They're very popular back home. Big machines. The Dean has one, and so do Alice and I. Hers is a bit older than mine and a bit unreliable now, but she'll get a few more years out of it, I believe. We have a great mechanic – Rosie. She can keep anything going.'

'Very interesting,' said von Igelfeld.

Pom Pom was looking bemused. 'I guess you don't know much about motorbikes. Am I right?'

Von Igelfeld shrugged. 'I know a bit, perhaps.'

'Like they've got two wheels?'

Von Igelfeld nodded. 'Oh, I know that.'

Pom Pom thought, *He's something else. Oh my! This is living, breathing history.* She cleared her throat. 'Have you been on a bike recently?'

Von Igelfeld hesitated. He had never been on a motorbike, but he did not want to say it. So he waved a hand carelessly. 'No, not recently.'

Pom Pom gestured towards the back of the building. 'I've got that Ducati out there. Do you fancy a trip down the road?'

Von Igelfeld looked out of the window. He was a professor of the University of Regensburg. He was a past chairman of the German Association of Philological Studies. He was a former Alexander von Humboldt Fellow. And here he was being offered a ride on a motorbike.

'I wouldn't mind,' he said.

'We can take a rain check on the tea,' said Pom Pom, getting to her feet.

'Oh yes,' said von Igelfeld. He was not sure what a rain check was, but he would be happy to take one if it meant that he could spend more time with this intriguing visitor. And she really was intriguing – rather like Circe, he thought, if one were to seek a classical analogy. Mind you, that was a bit unfair. Circe was an enchantress – Pom Pom was a scholar of the Provençal language. There was an important difference. Yet there was something enchanting about Professor Pom Pom Boisseau, he thought, and perhaps he was in a similar position to Odysseus's crewmen. Careful. Careful.

They left the building together. As they walked, von Igelfeld asked where Alice was. He was told that she was having something done downtown.

'Something done to her motorbike?' he asked.

'No,' said Pom Pom. 'She's getting a tattoo. She found a great tattoo parlour near the station. A real artist, she said. She's having a design done.'

Von Igelfeld stopped in his tracks. 'She's . . .' He struggled to find the words.

'Just a small one,' said Pom Pom. 'And very discreet. Where nobody will see it – or not many, shall we say.' With this, she gave von Igelfeld a wink.

'But . . .'

'You don't have any art yourself?' asked Pom Pom, and then answered her own question. 'I suppose you don't.'

'I have some paintings in my flat,' said von Igelfeld.

This brought a loud laugh from Pom Pom. 'Oh, you could be in stand-up, Moritz-Maria – you really could.'

'Thank you,' said von Igelfeld, unsure about what she meant, but assuming it was a compliment.

'We've got a show back in the States called the *Late-Night Show*. They would book you any time.' She paused. 'Would you like me to try? I know someone who knows someone who works on the show. I could have a word with her.'

Von Igelfeld smiled modestly. This really was very encouraging; he was used to rather formal relations with women – he sensed that they were, for some inexplicable reason, in awe of him, but Pom Pom's manner was quite different. She *likes* me, von Igelfeld said to himself, and the thought brought with it a feeling of warmth and security. She would obviously be an admirer of *Portuguese Irregular Verbs*, that went without saying, but he sensed that it was not just his scholarship that she thought highly of – it was him, too. And that was such a flattering thought. Perhaps he should go on this Late-Night Show that she mentioned; he would remind her of that some other time and suggest that she got in touch with her friend about it.

From a copious panier compartment on the Ducati, Pom Pom produced two motorcycle helmets and a couple of pairs of leather gloves. For herself, she had a tight-fitting leather over-suit that she zipped up over the clothes she was wearing. Von Igelfeld was provided with a red scarf and a set of motorcycle goggles. 'The wind dries your eyes,' she explained. 'These will stop that.' She smiled as she watched him fit the goggles. 'Very cool, Moritz-Maria,' she said appreciatively.

Von Igelfeld returned her smile. It felt good to be described as cool, which did not happen to him very much. In fact, it had never happened.

'You're very kind,' he said, slipping his hands into the leather gloves.

'If we come off,' she said, 'which of course is highly unlikely to happen, then those gloves would protect you from grazing your hands.'

Von Igelfeld nodded, as if he knew that well. 'Of course,' he said.

She mounted the bike and indicated where he should sit behind her. 'Have you done much biking before?' she asked.

He made a vague gesture with a gloved hand. 'Not much,' he said.

'You know that you must lean the way I lean,' Pom Pom said. 'People feel tempted to lean the other way, but you mustn't. Follow me. That's very important.'

'I know,' said von Igelfeld.

She started the bike's engine. To von Igelfeld it sounded impossibly loud, and he glanced up at the Institute windows to see if anybody was watching. A movement at Herr Huber's window revealed a flash of librarian; so Herr Huber was watching, which was all to the good. Poor Herr

Huber – nobody would ever call him cool, thought von Igelfeld. But he was a good man, nonetheless, ploughing his narrow furrow of librarianship, being as helpful as one could ever expect anybody in an ancillary calling to be. Herr Huber was just the sort of person whom the Recording Angel would be watching, thought von Igelfeld wryly, and his entry into heaven – if such a place existed – would surely be accompanied by fanfares. For he who is last shall be first ... wasn't there something to that effect?

They set off. Von Igelfeld had his arms around Pom Pom's waist, and he held on tightly to her leather suit as they shot down the road, weaving in and out of traffic. Reaching a main road, Pom Pom half turned her head and shouted over the wind, 'Ready to fly?'

Von Igelfeld shouted out a few words of encouragement. He was not quite sure what he said, but it had its effect.

Half an hour later, when they returned to the Institute, von Igelfeld climbed gingerly off the pillion seat of the Ducati and removed his helmet, goggles and gloves.

'That was ... ' He struggled to find an adjective. He had never experienced anything like it before, and he felt light-headed with excitement and pleasure.

'*Wunderbar*,' he said.

'Precisely,' Pom Pom agreed. '*Wunderbar* more or less says it.'

*

From his office window, Unterholzer watched with Herr Huber as the extraordinary scene unfolded in the car park below.

'I never thought I'd see such a thing,' said Herr Huber. 'But I suppose life is full of surprises.'

Unterholzer shook his head sadly. 'I've foreseen this for some time,' he said. 'It's been apparent to me that our dear colleague, Professor Dr Dr von Igelfeld is losing his reason. He made a very strange remark the other day about modal verbs in early English. I could hardly believe what I was hearing.'

Herr Huber frowned. 'But English is very strange, at the best of times,' he said.

'This went well beyond any of the normal quirkiness of that unfortunate language,' Unterholzer insisted. 'And then, in the library the other day, I heard him humming a few bars of Wagner to himself. That was very strange. I imagine that you do not encourage Wagner in the library, Herr Huber.'

Herr Huber did not give a direct answer, but it was obvious to Unterholzer that his supposition was correct.

Now Unterholzer continued, 'The first sign of mental imbalance, I'm told, is a lack of inhibition. Now, wouldn't you say, Herr Huber, that taking up motorcycling when you're in Professor von Igelfeld's position is a sign of a lack of inhibition?'

Herr Huber sighed. 'Yes, I suppose I would. It's such a pity.'

'And would you not further agree,' Unterholzer went on, 'that those of us who are still in possession of our faculties should take steps to help our poor deluded colleague?'

'Put that way,' said Herr Huber, 'I would say yes.'

'Which is why I must act,' said Unterholzer.

Herr Huber nodded his approval. 'Professor von Igelfeld is fortunate indeed to have a kind friend like you, Professor Dr Unterholzer. Of that, I am certain.'

'Thank you,' said Unterholzer. 'We must protect our colleagues, Herr Huber.'

'Indeed, we must,' said Herr Huber. He shook his head. 'Sometimes episodes of irrational behaviour are very short-lived. We must hope that this is one such.'

'But we should avoid the temptation to clutch at straws,' warned Unterholzer. 'I fear that this is not going to end well for our colleague.'

Herr Huber looked thoughtful. 'If Professor von Igelfeld is committed to hospital, I wonder what will happen to his room.'

Unterholzer looked a perfect picture of innocence. He looked up at the ceiling. 'I hadn't thought of that.'

For a few moments Herr Huber was silent. He knew that Unterholzer had wanted that room for a very long time, and now, it seemed, there was a prospect of his getting it. The dawning of that realisation led to another thought:

what if Unterholzer was planning to so arrange matters that von Igelfeld was falsely committed to a psychiatric hospital? These things were closely regulated these days, but evidence could be falsified. Presumably there were people languishing in state institutions who should not be there: no system was perfect, after all. Was von Igelfeld possibly being set up by ... An awful possibility suggested itself. That lady from Louisiana could be in league with Unterholzer whom, for all that anybody knew, she might have met at one of those conferences these people go to all the time. Unterholzer may have invited her to come to the Institute so that she might have the opportunity of luring von Igelfeld into a situation where he made himself a laughing stock. That would make the whole thing a conspiracy, and one had to be cautious about accusations of conspiracy. But some conspiracies really did exist, especially in circumstances where the stakes were extremely high – as they undoubtedly were in this case.

He looked at Unterholzer, who met his gaze without blinking. But that, thought Herr Huber, was what real plotters did: they were unflinching.

'I think we should be careful about jumping to conclusions,' Herr Huber said.

Unterholzer rolled his eyes. 'Herr Huber,' he said, drawing himself up to his full height. 'You will remember that I am a professor of this university. You are, and it is an honourable calling, a librarian. On academic matters, the opinion of librarians is sometimes sought, and is on many occasions most helpful. On other occasions, though, it is not required. I am not saying that this occasion is one such, but I am aware that there are some who might take that view. I only say this as an observation – nothing more.'

Herr Huber bit his lip, and said nothing. He was in a very awkward position, and he was not at all sure what to do. One thing was clear, though: he could not do nothing. Oh, this was a wretched situation, and it was all the fault of those two American professors. Why did they have to come here, with their motorbikes and all, and disturb the peace under which the Institute had for so long flourished? If they had not arrived, then von Igelfeld would never have lost his mind, if that is what had happened. Or was he simply in love with Professor Pom Pom Boisseau? *Amor furor brevis est*, said the ancients, and there were cases where that was probably true. But not everybody who fell head over heels for somebody else was for that reason insane. He himself was very fond of his wife, Frau Huber – in fact, he would readily say that he was in love with her. But that did not mean that he had, by virtue of that emotion, lost his reason.

Unterholzer was leaving. 'Don't say anything about this, Herr Huber,' he warned. 'We must try at all costs to avoid scandal – although I must admit that there will already be people who have seen Professor von Igelfeld on that motorbike with his hands on that lady's waist. Closing the stable door will do little to prevent the horse from bolting.'

Herr Huber absorbed this quietly. He did not want to give

any assurance that he would not say anything about what had happened, and he thought that perhaps it would be best if he subtly encouraged Unterholzer to leave his room. That would bring the conversation to an end. He had noticed that Unterholzer tended to become impatient when he spoke to him about the nursing home. For some inexplicable reason, he did not seem to be interested in that, and would make an excuse of having pressing business elsewhere when the topic was raised.

'Oh, by the way,' he began, 'I've been meaning to tell you about something I heard from one of the nursing staff when I visited my aunt. There is a lady there – a senior nurse – who comes from Bonn originally although she worked for several years in Berlin, where she met a man who was a fairly senior official in one of the ministries. This man told her that there was somebody in one of the Government press offices who quite deliberately . . . '

Unterholzer looked at his watch.

'Excuse me, Herr Huber,' he said. 'Another time.'

Herr Huber demurred, and Unterholzer left the room. It had worked. Now he could draft a letter to von Igelfeld, telling him to exercise caution. It would have to be anonymous, as it was just too embarrassing to speak to him face to face about a matter as delicate as this. Herr Huber had never imagined that he would find himself penning an anonymous letter, but these were extreme times and he really had no alternative.

Dear Professor von Igelfeld, he wrote. *I feel I must warn you that there are people who have seen you riding off on a motorbike with a well-built American lady dressed in leather. Forgive me for saying this, but you should be extremely careful. I have your interests at heart, and remain, as always, a Well-Wisher.*

He put the letter in an envelope and addressed it, using his left hand to disguise his handwriting. He would post it that evening after he had visited his aunt in the nursing home. It was a Wednesday, and they always had cauliflower cheese for lunch in the home on a Wednesday. Knowing how much her nephew liked it, Herr Huber's aunt would always keep a small helping of cauliflower cheese for him to eat when he came to visit her. She would present it to him on a saucer, saying 'And here's a little surprise for you', although it was never a surprise, as the same thing happened every Wednesday. But Herr Huber would affect not to have expected the treat and exclaim how much he enjoyed cauliflower cheese at any time of the day.

Herr Huber's Letter

At coffee the next morning, taken as usual in the small common room on the ground floor, there was at first an unusual atmosphere. The three professors were there, as they invariably were, although Prinzel announced that he would have to leave early, owing to a dental appointment. This broke any ice that there was, prompting Herr Huber to begin a lengthy and detailed story about his experience of root-canal treatment, a procedure that he said he would be loath to recommend even to his worst enemies.

Von Igelfeld was silent during this exchange – not because he had no view on root-canal treatment, nor out of sympathy for Prinzel, who might be subjected to such treatment within the hour, but because he had remembered how fond he had once been of his dentist. That came to nothing, as he had discovered that she was using the copy of *Portuguese Irregular Verbs* he had given her to stand on in order to improve her access to patients' mouths. That was an unfortunate memory, best forgotten, and yet it tended to come to mind whenever dentists were mentioned.

Herr Huber's dental reflections were followed by a brief, non-contentious discussion of an editorial point that had arisen around the forthcoming issue of the *Zeitschrift*. That lasted until it was time for Prinzel to go off for his dental appointment. Shortly after that, when Herr Huber was summoned by one of his assistants to take a phone call, Unterholzer and von Igelfeld were left alone in the common room.

Unterholzer stared into his coffee cup. Then, after a few moments he said, 'It appears that our current visitors are settling in well. They seem happy enough, don't you think, Professor Dr Dr (*honoris causa*) von Igelfeld?'

The term of address used by Unterholzer was significant. The two scholars had known one another for years, and had technically moved to the stage of allowing the use of first names. But Unterholzer had never been comfortable with the use of Moritz-Maria, and, for his part, von Igelfeld had never been able to take Unterholzer's own first names at all seriously. There was discomfort on both sides, but that alone did not justify the reversion to the full academic title that Unterholzer had now used: *Herr* von Igelfeld would have been quite appropriate in the circumstances. That, at least, would have avoided the sting implicit in leaving out the *mult* after von Igelfeld's honorary doctorates. Everybody knew – and that included Unterholzer – that von Igelfeld now had three honorary doctorates, and that this justified the use of *mult*, even if one took the view – and opinion was genuinely divided on this – that the possession of three honorary doctorates was insufficient grounds for the use of the term.

Von Igelfeld took the slight in his stride. Unterholzer could be moody, and there was no point in engaging with him over so small – well, relatively small – a matter.

'I think we are very fortunate to have them,' von Igelfeld said, his voice remaining even. 'I believe that they are planning to give a presentation on the latest theories of the migration of Provençal. Professor Boisseau tells me that there have been some interesting developments in that area.'

Unterholzer nodded politely. So that was what they discussed as they sped down the road on that ghastly red motorbike. What else? Of course, they would have been talking about Provençal. He bit his tongue. He would have to be careful: any attempt at a wry observation might just push von Igelfeld over the edge. He decided to mention something altogether different.

'Our visitors were telling me,' he began, 'about one of their colleagues at Tulane. He is a certain Professor la Fouche, who is well known in the field of non-human communication.'

Von Igelfeld showed polite interest, but nothing more.

'Whales, and so on?' he asked. 'Whales communicate over vast distances, I believe.' He paused. 'I have not heard them personally, you must understand.'

'No,' said Unterholzer. 'This is oyster communication. He has studied oysters for many years.'

Von Igelfeld smiled. 'I have *eaten* oysters for many years,' he quipped.

Unterholzer looked pained. This was not a moment for levity. 'He has written a very important paper on how oysters pass information on to one another.'

'In a tight-lipped way?' said von Igelfeld.

Unterholzer ignored this. 'I'm right,' he said to himself. 'Von Igelfeld is becoming increasingly deranged – these odd interjections are the proof.

He abandoned the discussion of oysters. 'I noticed that you had a ride on her motorbike yesterday,' he remarked, trying to sound as casual as possible.

He had not been sure how von Igelfeld would take this, but he was surprised when it elicited a broad smile.

'I did indeed,' said von Igelfeld. 'We went very fast. In fact, we overtook many cars. Pom Pom is a very competent biker.'

Unterholzer's lips tightened. 'You're lucky you didn't fall off, don't you think?'

'There was no danger of that,' said von Igelfeld airily. And then, without warning, he asked, 'Are you enjoying that new book by Professor Fantozzi?'

Unterholzer frowned. He had not yet opened the book,

Herr Huber's Letter

which was still sitting on his desk, and therefore was unaware of the chapter it contained on *Portuguese Irregular Verbs*. He was surprised that von Igelfeld knew that he had the book, and even as he thought about this, he realised that Herr Huber must have told him. This was serious. A librarian had no business telling one member of the Institute what another was reading. That information could be sensitive, as it might reveal the direction of a scholar's work. The world of academic research could be competitive, particularly when it came to applications for grants, and it was perfectly possible to imagine circumstances in which one would not want a colleague to know about some inchoate piece of research.

Really, thought Unterholzer, Herr Huber was impossible. He could not keep his mouth shut – not for one moment, it seemed. That was troubling, but equally troubling was why von Igelfeld should suddenly be expressing an interest in this book by that obscure Italian professor from Bari, or Messina, or one of those impossible places in the south of Italy, where anything could happen, and frequently did.

'I'm finding the book quite intriguing,' Unterholzer answered, in guarded tones. 'It is always interesting to know what our Italian colleagues are up to. They are so energetic in so many different ways.'

Von Igelfeld knew immediately that Unterholzer had not opened the book, and certainly that he had not discovered the chapter that was so complimentary about his own work.

'I wonder if I might take a look at it,' he said. 'I'd only need it for a couple of hours.' Long enough, he thought, to photocopy the entire work, if not just the relevant chapter.

Unterholzer hesitated. He clearly had to humour von Igelfeld, but there were limits. He had borrowed that book, and was entitled to keep it for six weeks. Those were the rules. And von Igelfeld was clearly up to something, anyway, and would have to be resisted.

'I shall be returning it to Herr Huber in six weeks,' he said calmly. 'I'm sure that he will make a note to let you know when it is back in the library.'

Von Igelfeld listened, his expression impassive. This was typical Unterholzer. He was so selfish and dog-in-the-manger-ish. He must have picked up that attitude from that ridiculous dog of his.

'Oh well,' said von Igelfeld, rising to his feet. 'I'd better return to work. And you'll need to get back to Professor Fantozzi's excellent book. It must be difficult for you to tear yourself away from it.'

Unterholzer thought quickly. He had been hoping for a pretext to invite von Igelfeld to dinner so that his wife's cousin Klaus-Peter could make an assessment of his mental state. Now he saw how he might get him there. 'On the subject of our visitors,' he said, 'Frau Unterholzer and I were proposing to invite our American visitors for dinner at our house. I wonder whether you would care to join us.'

Von Igelfeld immediately forgot about Professor Fantozzi and his book. An invitation to dinner *chez Unterholzer* would provide an opportunity to spend more time in the company of Pom Pom. He accepted immediately – even though he knew that Frau Unterholzer served outstandingly dull fare. How many things could you do with a potato? She certainly had twenty or thirty potato-based recipes up her sleeve.

'Good,' said Unterholzer. 'I have yet to talk to our American colleagues, but I shall do so soon. We can then fix a date. It will be very pleasant, I think, Herr von Igelfeld?'

The shift in terms of address indicated a thawing of the earlier ice, and von Igelfeld responded appropriately. 'You are most kind, Detlev Amadeus.'

'Thank you, Moritz-Maria,' said Unterholzer. 'Of course, if they are unable to make it because of a previous engagement, then we can still have dinner ourselves – a diminished party, but there we are.'

Von Igelfeld struggled to conceal his immediate reaction to this. On the last occasion on which he had had dinner at the Unterholzer house, there had been that most unfortunate incident with a bottle of olive oil. A considerable time had elapsed since then, yet the memory of that awful moment was still painful. But the key to equanimity, he believed, was to put the past behind us and not allow it to clutter up the present. That was why some languages had a specific construction for events that had happened a long time ago and that were of no further relevance to the affairs of the present. One day he would write a paper on the subject, and use as an example, suitably anonymised, of course, Unterholzer's occasional bringing up of the misfortunes of his sausage dog, Walter. Perhaps there was a case for the development of a *past trivial* tense, which would refer to things that were so trivial as to merit complete forgetting. That was not the way language developed – unfortunately. Language evolved in the stomachs of the living, in the usage of ordinary people who were, for the most part, misinformed and wrong about so much.

Von Igelfeld sighed. The French had the right idea, entrusting the guardianship of the language to the *Académie Française*. The limitation with their arrangements, though, was the inability of the Academy to prosecute people for the use of unauthorised loan-words or for unapproved neologisms. The results were plain to see: the French language, once the strict Alexandrine muse of Racine, a glory every bit as impressive as Versailles, was now littered with meaningless expressions (*vachement* being an example); with meaningless sounds that people uttered to express their insouciance; or with countless subversive words such as *bouffer*, which was replacing *manger*, or *pote*, which was used instead of *ami*. If the *Académie Française* were to be

Herr Huber's Letter

only slightly more vigilant, these things could be nipped in the bud before they transformed the language out of all recognition.

Von Igelfeld now said, 'I hope that they will be able to join us, or at least that Pom Pom will ...' He stopped himself. He saw that Unterholzer was looking at him with a peculiar, alert expression.

Von Igelfeld corrected himself. 'It would be a great pity if only one of them was able to come to dinner.'

Precisely, thought Unterholzer: a pity *for you*. He gave von Igelfeld an intense stare, one that was as much composed of sympathy as it was of foreboding. So might a sensitive assassin – if such a person were ever to exist – look upon a nominated victim, knowing that the victim does not deserve what is coming.

Because von Igelfeld's mind had been on other matters – such is the distracting power of infatuation – there was a pile of unanswered correspondence waiting on his desk. Returning to his office after this conversation with Unterholzer, he sat down to deal with this, his heart sinking at the sight of the numerous brown official envelopes that concealed various circulars from university bureaucrats. They were always going on about things like safety precautions and awareness training, and matters of that sort, and it was von Igelfeld's habit to throw most of them immediately into the bin. That irritating Herr Uber-Huber was a major offender in this regard. He had had the temerity recently to remind staff that they were entitled to a mere five weeks of holiday a year, and that they should not go off and live abroad from late spring until early autumn. How dare he, thought von Igelfeld. What academic staff did with their time was their business and none of the concern of what Herr Uber-Huber presumed to call the Department of Human Resources. Naturally, he described himself as Uber-Director of that department, another of those director titles that had no foundation in the University's ancient constitution. If I ever became Rector of the University, von Igelfeld thought, the first task I would tackle would be to clean out the Augean Stables that was the University administration. One of the first to go would be Herr Uber-Huber, although mercy would, of course, be shown, and he would not be arbitrarily dismissed. Instead, he would be offered a post as a groundsman, perhaps, driving one of those sit-on lawnmowers that people drove across large expanses of grass. That would give him plenty of time to contemplate the error of interfering with academic convention. Or he could be given a job assisting Frau Schlaginhauffen in the canteen, perhaps keeping an inventory of her famous *Münchner Weisswurst*. That would bring him down to earth soon enough.

For a few moments, von Igelfeld allowed himself the pleasure of imagining Herr Uber-Huber dressed in a white apron with one of those curious white paper hats that food-handlers wear. It was a delicious picture, but he was not a vindictive man, and he quickly brought the fantasy to an end. Herr Uber-Huber was only doing his best; he was, like so many people one came across, simply misguided – a category of persons one might call the *conscientious misguided*, not that different from the group labelled by doctors as the *worried well*. The conscientious misguided did not deserve to be punished in any way – they simply needed to be shown how wrong they were and helped to see the error of their ways. There was still hope for Herr Uber-Huber.

Although there were no letters from Herr Uber-Huber in the pile confronting von Igelfeld, there was one letter that stood out. Unlike most of the others, which were slit open as a matter of course by von Igelfeld's secretary, Frau Froeschle, this letter was untouched, having the word *Personal* written prominently, if in a rather shaky hand, above the address.

He examined the envelope before opening it – a superstitious ritual that had survived since childhood, when he would always hold letters up to the light before opening them. Sometimes one might see the contents – an occasional banknote from an uncle, for instance – or be able to make out print or handwriting if the envelope was made of sufficiently flimsy paper. In this case there were no clues on the outside – no sender name or return address – and the paper of which the envelope was made was completely opaque. Hesitantly, he slit it open.

It was Herr Huber's anonymous letter. Von Igelfeld read it twice before lowering it to the table. Who was the 'well-wisher' and why had he taken it upon himself to write in such alarmist terms? He had never received an anonymous letter before, and could not conceive of why anybody should single him out for the receipt of one. He pondered this, and then frowned. There was something familiar about this letter – something in the wording that made him think he might know the author.

He concentrated on one sentence, where the author began *Forgive me for saying this*, and ended *I remain, as always*... What had started as a vague suspicion now became a certainty: these two expressions made the authorship of the letter as clear as if there had been a signature, followed by the spelling out of the author's name in block capitals. There was only one person known to von Igelfeld who regularly used both of these expressions, and that person was Herr Huber. In particular, every letter that Herr Huber wrote, every circular that he sent to von Igelfeld and others, ended with *I remain, as always*... Nobody else said that any longer; nobody.

Von Igelfeld shook his head in disbelief. He had no doubt now but that Herr Huber was responsible for this anonymous letter, but he was completely in the dark as to why he should have written it. If he felt that there was something he should warn von Igelfeld about, then surely the answer would have been to raise the matter with him. After all, they saw one another several times every day, and there would have been no shortage of opportunities to speak, even on a matter as confidential as this one appeared to be.

He had puzzled over this for several minutes before a disturbing thought came to him. Was Herr Huber undergoing some sort of mid-life crisis? Von Igelfeld had heard that middle-aged men could behave erratically as they saw youthfulness slip away behind them. It was some sort of desperation, and it lent an irrational flavour to their conduct. Of course, he himself would never be so afflicted, but it was entirely possible that poor Herr Huber, on contemplating his lot in life, might decide that success had passed him by and that all that lay ahead was slow decline. Perhaps Herr Huber had never really wanted to be Herr Huber, Librarian of the Institute of Romance Philology. Perhaps he had long dreamed of being Herr Huber, international businessman; or Colonel Huber, aviator *extraordinaire* and head of the *Luftwaffenführungsdienstkommando;* or even a sought-after Siegfried at Bayreuth. The fact that he was none of those things, and that his life was so predictable and circumscribed, might just have tipped him, in a moment or madness, into writing anonymous letters about imaginary threats. Poor Herr Huber, who was so harmless; who was such a familiar part of the Institute's furniture; who was so dutiful in his devotion to his elderly aunt in her nursing home; who was, von Igelfeld believed, a considerate and loyal husband to the wife with whom he shared that almost Hansel-and-Gretel-like cottage at the edge of the woods – he was not somebody to be upbraided at all, but gently helped to find the counselling and support that would enable him to get through his mid-life crisis.

Von Igelfeld wondered what he should do. The University made a point of stressing that it had psychiatric support facilities for members of staff who were under stress. There had recently been a long circular to that effect from Herr Uber-Huber, in his capacity as Human Resources Director, and although von Igelfeld had not been slow to throw it in the wastepaper bin, the first few lines had caught his attention. *If you or somebody with whom you work,* the circular read, *are feeling overwhelmed, do not wait for the problem to become more serious. Our staff of counsellors are here to help. Do not be embarrassed to call for our confidential assistance . . .* Von Igelfeld had not considered this to be relevant to anybody working in the Institute of Romance Philology, but now he was not so sure. He would have a word with Herr Uber-Huber, perhaps, and gently apprise him of the fact that his near-namesake in the Institute was clearly overwhelmed. It was the least he could do for Herr Huber, who was a good man, in spite of everything, who did his best, which, ultimately, was the most that any of us could be expected to do. They did not make innocent, courteous men like Herr

Huber any longer, thought von Igelfeld – the Librarian belonged to a vanishing Germany, a country that was becoming more and more remote, a land from which the radio signals were daily fainter and fainter, distant echoes in the ether, punctuated by long silences.

An Important Man

Von Igelfeld tried to put out of his mind altogether Professor Fantozzi's book. He knew that he would be able to see it in the fullness of time, even if he had to wait six weeks, and until then he would be patient. That was what he hoped, but in the event his eagerness to read what the Italian scholar had said about *Portuguese Irregular Verbs* proved too much for him. Now he made his decision: he would pay a visit to the politician who, according to Herr Huber, had the power to change University regulations. If that were true, he would ask him to allow the variation of the six-week rule behind which Unterholzer, in all his selfishness, was sheltering. It seemed absurd that he had to go to such lengths to deal with something as minor as a library rule, but if that was what was required, then that was what he would do. And there was a point of general principle here, he thought: the ethos of scholarship, as practised in places like the Institute, was that one scholar should help another in the spirit of the free exchange of information. It was *not* that a person should be allowed to prevent others from consulting a book that was, after all, the property of the Institute. He would explain that to the politician in question, and he would be bound to see it from von Igelfeld's point of view. It was unfortunate if Unterholzer could only be defeated by such a strategy, but von Igelfeld had tried making a civil and reasonable request and had been rebuffed for his pains. That left him with no alternative, and there was not a court in the land, von Igelfeld thought, that would take a contrary view.

So it was that von Igelfeld telephoned to make an appointment with Herr Andreas Durchdenwald. The politician's secretary proved both charming and obliging, and two days later von Igelfeld found himself standing outside the suite of offices shared by Herr Durchdenwald and several other representatives of his particular party, the German Progress Alliance. This was not a party about which von Igelfeld knew very much, other than that they were an alliance that operated at a national level and believed in progress. Well, he believed in progress too, and he imagined that he and Herr Durchdenwald would therefore see eye to eye on a whole range of matters, including the need to reform library regulations.

Von Igelfeld was shown into a waiting room. 'Herr Durchdenwald is currently on the line to Berlin,' the secretary explained, pausing to underline the weightiness of being on the line to Berlin. 'He will not be long, and once he has finished – with the Minister – then he will be delighted to see you.'

'Ah,' said von Igelfeld. 'With the Minister ... I certainly wouldn't want to interrupt that.'

The secretary smiled. 'Herr Durchdenwald is always willing to talk to ordinary people too, not just Government ministers ... in Berlin.'

Von Igelfeld smiled. 'That is very progressive,' he said.

The secretary nodded her agreement, and then returned to her office. Von Igelfeld sat down and stared at the noticeboard that occupied almost an entire wall. On it were pinned various cut-out newspaper articles, illustrated in many cases with pictures of Herr Durchdenwald engaged in various constituency activities. Here he was planting a tree in a public park, watched by a group of ladies in floral dresses and wide-brimmed summer hats; here he was reviewing a group of boy scouts, all dressed in lederhosen, lined up in front of a tent; here he was standing with a group of catering workers outside a well-known hotel. Then there were press articles on his achievements. *Durchi saves community!* boasted one headline, reporting his successful prevention of the building of a new road through a small village. He was clearly a busy man, thought von Igelfeld, and he hoped that this business of library regulations would not be beneath his notice. And yet, even if it would appear small to an outsider, to von Igelfeld it was a matter of grave importance. Would Durchi understand that? von Igelfeld asked himself.

The Lost Language of Oysters

He did not have to wait long to meet the great man. After five minutes or so, the door through which the secretary had retreated opened and Herr Andreas Durchdenwald peered into the room.

'Professor von Igelfeld?' he asked.

Von Igelfeld stood up and moved across the room to shake hands with the politician.

Then, after Herr Durchdenwald's invitation to follow him, he made his way into an office at the end of a short corridor.

'My workplace,' announced Herr Durchdenwald. 'Not palatial, but very convenient in other respects.'

'An office is just a place to work in,' said von Igelfeld. 'A desk and a chair are all one really needs.'

'And a carpet,' added Herr Durchdenwald. 'In Government circles, one's seniority is reflected in the size of one's carpet. It's said that the *Bundeskanzler* has two carpets: one underneath the other.' Herr Durchdenwald smiled. 'Of course, he has to tread softly around many issues.'

Von Igelfeld looked puzzled. 'I see no need for two carpets, personally. How much more important it is to have a good-sized bookcase.'

Herr Durchdenwald laughed. 'If one has time to read – since I took office I never seem to be in that position. I suppose you read most of the day – in your line of work.' He paused. 'What do you teach, by the way?'

Von Igelfeld hesitated. He taught very little, and only

mounted one or two occasional seminars for students. 'Ours is principally a research institute,' he said.

'Of course,' said Herr Durchdenwald. 'Research is very important if we are to maintain our competitive edge with other countries. More research – that's what I always say. We must do more research.' He gave von Igelfeld an enquiring look. 'In what field is your research, Professor von Igelfeld?'

Von Igelfeld hesitated. People often seemed not to appreciate what Romance Philology was all about, and he was not sure that Herr Durchdenwald would do so. He was a fairly bluff sort of man, in appearance at least – not somebody whom you would suspect understood finer scholarly issues. That did not bode well, of course, for his grasp of the library issue, but that would become apparent in due course.

'Language,' said von Igelfeld.

'Which language?' asked Herr Durchdenwald.

'Many languages,' replied von Igelfeld. 'I am the author of a work on Portuguese irregular verbs.'

Herr Durchdenwald looked interested. 'A Portuguese phrase book? Perhaps I should buy a copy. As it happens, our daughter is marrying a young man from Portugal and we want to show willing when it comes to meeting our future in-laws.'

'It's not really a phrase book,' said von Igelfeld.

'Oh well,' said Herr Durchdenwald. 'I'm sure we shall find something that serves our purpose. Portuguese *sounds* so odd, doesn't it? All those nasal, sniffing sounds. I always think that Portuguese people sound as if they want to blow their nose. But I suppose they don't. Well, some of them may need to blow their noses – but for ordinary reasons – it's nothing to do with the language.'

This observation was followed by a brief silence. Then Herr Durchdenwald continued, 'My secretary said that you wanted to speak to me about a very important matter. Would you care to tell me about it?'

Von Igelfeld went straight to the point. 'There is a university regulation that needs changing. I gather that you can arrange the necessary ministerial approval for this.'

Herr Durchdenwald nodded. 'I'm often asked to arrange for the ben . . . '

He stopped himself, but von Igelfeld had already decided that he had been about to say 'for the bending of the rules'. Now he sought to reassure him. 'I do not want any rules bent, Herr Durchdenwald,' he said, trying not to sound too disapproving. 'I would simply ask for what one might call a *variation*.'

'Yes, a variation,' said Herr Durchdenwald. 'That sounds much better. And I'm sure that I'll be able to arrange things for you.'

Von Igelfeld's eyes opened wide. This was an excellent outcome – and the meeting had only just started. He would hardly have dared to imagine that Herr Durchdenwald would be so obliging, but here he was, more or less suggesting that any request would be met. Were all politicians this helpful, or was it something to do with the fact that Herr Durchdenwald was a member of the German Progress Alliance party? As the name suggested, this was a party that believed in progress – and the reform of library regulations was certainly a matter of progress.

'Yes,' said Herr Durchdenwald. 'These administrative variations are usually no problem – with the right backing, of course. And that is where I can claim to come in.'

'You are very kind,' said von Igelfeld.

Herr Durchdenwald smiled at this. 'It's not a question of kindness – not always. Although I must say that I do try to be helpful.' He paused. 'What do you know of our particular party, Professor von Igelfeld?'

'You're progressive,' answered von Igelfeld. 'I think your name implies that. And I imagine that means you are forward-looking.'

Herr Durchdenwald acknowledged the compliment. 'Thank you. We believe in the future. The future is where . . . where things are going to happen.'

Von Igelfeld considered this. It was, he decided, undeniably true.

'But running a political party,' Herr Durchdenwald went on, 'is of course a difficult business.'

'I can imagine so,' said von Igelfeld. 'And I don't think you'll get much thanks for it.'

Herr Durchdenwald was very much in agreement with that. 'You certainly don't,' he said. 'People complain and criticise. They love finding fault with anything you do – anything. If some people are to be believed, nothing we do is any good. Moan, moan, moan: it's what some people do all the time.'

It was the same in Romance Philology, von Igelfeld thought.

'But,' continued Herr Durchdenwald, 'there are compensations. You get things done. You help individual constituents – such as yourself – and then you find that they help you. Politics, you see, is a reciprocal business. You do a favour for somebody – and you get a favour in return.'

Von Igelfeld said that he thought much of life was like that. 'Reciprocity is important,' he said. 'I am on the editorial board of an academic journal – our own *Zeitschrift* at the Institute. We find that if we review somebody's book in our journal, then we can expect a review of our own books in their journal. It often happens that way.'

Herr Durchdenwald agreed enthusiastically. 'Precisely. That's exactly the way it works.'

Von Igelfeld waited. It seemed to him that Herr Durchdenwald had something else to say and he did not want to interrupt.

At length the silence was broken. 'I have great admiration for the University,' Herr Durchdenwald said.

'I'm very pleased to hear that,' said von Igelfeld.

'I have a son,' Herr Durchdenwald continued. 'Maximilian. He is eighteen next month.'

'That is a major milestone in one's life,' said von Igelfeld.

'Oh, it is. I remember the milestones. *Als ich ein kleiner Junge war* ... I had no idea then that I would end up in politics. I wanted to be a production engineer.'

'A very important profession,' said von Igelfeld. 'There are many challenges in production engineering.'

'Yes.'

Another short silence ensued. Then Herr Durchdenwald disclosed that Maximilian was hoping to study production engineering. 'I have encouraged him,' he said. 'I haven't done so just to fulfil my own unfulfilled ambition – it's not like that.'

'I'm sure it isn't,' von Igelfeld assured him. 'But it must be very satisfying when one sees one's dreams being acted out by one's offspring.' He paused. 'Which university is he hoping to attend, Herr Durchdenwald?'

The reply came quickly. 'This one. Right here. Regensburg.'

Von Igelfeld smiled. 'A very good choice, I imagine.' He tried to remember if he had met any of the professors of engineering. There was a Professor Schmidt, who taught something like that, and who had served with von Igelfeld on a university committee some years earlier, but he might have been chemistry, come to think of it. He had talked about his laboratory, von Igelfeld seemed to recall, which suggested chemistry rather than engineering. But it was difficult to tell with these people, he thought.

'Yes,' said Herr Durchdenwald. 'It is a good choice from many points of view. He will be able to lodge with us, you see, and that will make for a very substantial saving.'

'Yes,' said von Igelfeld. 'And you will know that he is being well cared for.'

Herr Durchdenwald stroked his chin. 'Of course, that is all based on the assumption that he gets a place. I gather it's very competitive.'

Von Igelfeld nodded. 'I am sure that he will be all right.'

Herr Durchdenwald looked doubtful. 'His school record doesn't reflect his ability, in my view. He was a bit distracted by sporting commitments. He's very good at football, you see.'

Von Igelfeld said nothing.

'I don't think he actually meets the entry requirements,' Herr Durchdenwald went on, adding, 'not if one takes a strict view of the situation. However ... '

Again, von Igelfeld waited. He noticed that Herr Durchdenwald was looking at him intensely. It was rather unsettling.

'Yes,' said Herr Durchdenwald at last. 'It would be such a pity if a talent like that – for engineering, that is – were not to be given a chance. A real pity – and all because of some ridiculous rule.' He paused. 'Rather like this rule you're wanting changed – or shall I say, interpreted in a more *sympathetic* manner.'

In the ensuing silence, von Igelfeld became aware

of the ticking of a clock. He looked up, beyond Herr Durchdenwald's head, to see a large round clock on the wall, the sort of clock one used to see at minor railway stations. A second hand jerked its way round the face, marking the passage of time between the statement and response in this increasingly uncomfortable conversation.

Herr Durchdenwald fiddled with a pencil, tapping it gently against the surface of his desk – a counterpoint to the ticking of the clock. Von Igelfeld looked pointedly at the pencil, but the politician seemed indifferent to the reproach.

'Of course, there is often a way round these minor bumps in the road, Professor von Igelfeld. So, if, for example, somebody within the University – some person of influence, shall we say, were to have a word with some other person, also within the University – some person connected with the admission process – and were to suggest to that person, that is, the person who plays a role in admission – who decides on admission, indeed – that in this particular case the student – that is, the student seeking admission – effectively my son, Maximilian, in fact – were to be given a place on the grounds of what one might call *prospective qualification*, which means that a young person is assessed not on what he has already achieved in school examinations – an unreliable test in many cases, it is sometimes suggested – but on the basis of what he is *likely* to achieve in the future, then the result would be, in an overall sense, satisfactory from all points of view, in as much as Maximilian would be given a place strictly on the grounds of merit, the emphasis throughout having been on *prospective* or *future* merit – an outcome, surely, that would satisfy the requirements of proper process and, I venture to say, distributive justice.' Herr Durchdenwald drew breath. 'In other words, you fix this for me, and I fix whatever it is you want fixed – not that I would describe the whole process in such reductionist terms, but one might just put it that way in order to ensure that nobody was in any doubt about what was going on.'

Von Igelfeld stared at Herr Durchdenwald without blinking. This was outrageous. It was one thing for him to approach this politician about an entirely justifiable recalibration of a library regulation, but it was quite another to suggest that improper influence be used to secure a university place for this youth, Maximilian Durchdenwald, who appeared to be more interested in football than academic matters. This was ... well, not to put too fine a point on it, corruption, and the very thought of a von Igelfeld, a scion of an ancient German family of noble traditions, participating in such a grubby exercise was abhorrent. And he imagined what he would have to do, were he to agree to this proposal. He would have to seek out a university bureaucrat of some sort, possibly even Herr Uber-Huber himself, and ask him to exercise favouritism. And Herr Uber-Huber, or his equivalent, would at that moment see that any moral claims of the von Igelfeld family, any assertion of nobility, any armorial claims, everything in fact, was built on sand, and that a von Igelfeld was no better than an Uber-Huber or the like. Oh, that would be a dark, dark avenue down which he would never venture, even if it meant having to wait six weeks before he could read the Fantozzi book on to which Unterholzer was so selfishly holding. This was all Unterholzer's fault; it was Unterholzer who had put him in this position of potential moral compromise.

But it was not too late to reject, in the clearest terms, this Siren voice.

'No,' said von Igelfeld. 'That is completely out of the question. The admission requirements of the University exist for a reason, and that reason is to set proper standards for those who are admitted to study.' He paused. 'I very much regret that I am unable to help you in this matter, Herr Durchdenwald, but I do hope that you will nonetheless be able to assist me in my entirely reasonable request.'

Herr Durchdenwald sat back in his chair. Von Igelfeld thought that his complexion had changed – or perhaps it was just the light that made him appear a bit redder than he had previously been. Now he spoke slowly and quietly. 'Professor von Igelfeld, I must say that I have no idea what you are referring to when you talk about university admission procedures. I cannot understand why you brought them up.'

'But *you* brought them up,' protested von Igelfeld.

Herr Durchdenwald shook his head. 'I fear that you misunderstood what I was saying. I was simply telling you about my son, Maximilian. I said nothing about university admission requirements.'

Von Igelfeld struggled to maintain his composure. 'You're mistaken, Herr Durchdenwald. You said ... '

And it was at this point that Herr Durchdenwald put down the pencil with which he had been fiddling in such an annoying way, and looked at his watch. 'Goodness me,' he said. 'How time flies. I must beg you to allow me to bring our most agreeable chat to an end. It has been very kind of you, dear Professor von Igelfeld, to come to talk to me about the progressive agenda of our party.'

Von Igelfeld rose to his feet. He was, of course, a tall man, as all von Igelfelds had been for several hundred years. Now he used his height to cast a reproachful look at Herr Durchdenwald, a somewhat shorter man. The glance seemed to have no effect.

'Wonderful weather,' said Herr Durchdenwald. He smiled. '*Auf wiedersehen*, as they say. Incidentally, what's goodbye in Portuguese? That's a word I really should acquire. Along with the Portuguese for *progressive*, of course.'

Picnic Thoughts

Winding their way between two orchards, the roar of their engines reverberating against the banks on either side of the narrow road, Professor Pom Pom Boisseau and Professor Alice Martinique rode their motorbikes towards the spot by a small river where they planned to have a picnic to celebrate Alice's birthday. Pom Pom had made a preliminary trip to the explore the site's potential, and had reported back to Alice that it was ideal. 'There's an oak tree that will provide shade,' she said, 'and the grass has recently been cut for hay. There's a field – Elysian – and a forest straight out of Humperdinck on the other side of the river.'

'Perfect,' said Alice. 'What does Omar Khayyam say? A book of verses underneath the bough/ A jug of wine, a loaf of bread/ And thou ... '

Pom Pom said that there would be no jug of wine, no loaf of bread, and probably no book of verses. 'But apart from that, I'll be there, sure.'

They turned off the road they were following and into a field. The bikes parked behind a hedge, they walked across a field to the place that Pom Pom had identified as their picnic spot. There, under the shade of the oak tree, they laid a red travel rug over the grass, put down the hamper they had transported in Pom Pom's rucksack, and unpacked their picnic lunch.

'I can't believe we're here,' said Pom Pom, as she sipped on the glass of lemonade that Alice had poured for her.

'Here, as in, in this field, under this oak tree?' asked Alice. 'Or as in Germany?'

'Germany,' said Pom Pom.

Alice smiled. 'A stroke of luck. That great office. That library. The delicious Herr Huber ... '

'Oh, Herr Huber!' exclaimed Pom Pom. 'He's so sweet, that man. I'm his major fangirl. I could just pick him up and put him in my display cabinet. They'd love him back in New Orleans.'

'Yes,' said Alice. 'Who wouldn't? I just love fussy men. You've heard him going on about his aunt and her nursing home?'

'Several times,' said Pom Pom.

'And he showed me a picture of his place on the edge of the woods. It looks as if it's made of gingerbread and candies.'

Pom Pom took a sip of her lemonade. 'I love non-threatening men. I imagine he does all the housework at home. And the cooking too.'

'So *mignon*.'

Pom Pom said, 'I can't wait to meet her – Frau Huber.'

'A little mouse. *This* size.'

Pom Pom laughed. 'We'd have to be careful not to sit on her by mistake. We'd have to say, "Oh, Herr Huber, I'm really sorry, but I've just sat on your wife."'

'And the others,' Alice said. 'Florianus Prinzel – what do you make of him?'

'Prussian type,' said Pom Pom. 'Uptight name – Prinzel. Bad *feng shui* there. Strict toilet training, I imagine.'

'And there's something weird about the tip of his nose. Have you noticed it?'

Pom Pom had not, and Alice explained. 'There's a very small scar – you have to peer to see it. I was doing that, and he noticed me. He turned away and blushed. I felt awful. Nobody likes to be caught staring at the tip of somebody else's nose. But it's as if it had fallen off at some point and been sewn back on. But not in quite the right place.'

'Odd,' said Pom Pom. 'I must take a closer look next time.'

'And Professor Unterholzer. He's called Detlev Amadeus.'

'Ridiculous,' said Pom Pom. 'But I suppose your name is one of the few things you can't help.'

'Of course, but still . . .' Alice broke off. 'And then there's your Moritz-Maria von Igelfeld. Talk about being German. He's *seriously* German, that one. *Echt.* The real thing.'

Pom Pom frowned. '*My* Moritz-Maria?'

Alice gave her a sideways look. 'Well, you and your Professor Dr Dr *und so weiter* ... You took him off on your bike. Don't think I didn't see you.' A note of petulance crept into her voice. 'I see things, you know.'

A sudden chill descended. It was a warm day and the air was sultry. In the distance there was a slight heat haze – a shimmering of blue. And yet there, under the shade of that oak, with crickets screeching somewhere in the undergrowth, the temperature seemed to drop several degrees.

Pom Pom's voice was a deep one – now it became even deeper. 'I took him for a ride because he had expressed an interest in the bikes. And he's our host – sort of.'

Alice did not meet her eye. 'Going off like that without telling me.'

Pom Pom shook her head. 'I thought you were still at the tattoo parlour.'

'You encouraged him, Pom Pom. I saw it all. I'd come back early. I was sore.' She paused. 'From my art. And I wanted to show you the new design and you weren't there. Why not? Because you were down the road with your new German friend. You didn't want to know about my new tattoo.'

Somewhere overhead a bird sang out. Pom Pom looked up. She did not want the picnic ruined. This, after all, was Alice's birthday. She realised she would have to make an effort.

'I assure you, Al,' she said. 'I really do. I was just trying to be nice to him. He's kind of cute, yes, but a lot of people are kind of cute in their Germanic sort of way. They can't help it.'

Alice sniffed.

'These people are our company,' Pom Pom continued. 'And von Igelfeld's written that book. You have to give it to him. The guy's a major figure.'

Alice sniffed again. 'I suppose so.'

'And it's your birthday,' continued Pom Pom.

'I know,' said Alice. 'Forty-five.' Her voice wavered as she repeated herself. 'Forty-five.'

'That's a great age to be,' said Pom Pom. She reached across the picnic rug to rest her hand on Alice's shoulder. 'So, tell me about your new art. I'm sorry I didn't ask.'

'I don't feel like talking about it right now,' Alice replied.

'No? Well, don't. Let's just enjoy this picnic. Nature. The sky. Being alive. The lot.'

Alice unwrapped a sandwich and passed it to Pom Pom. 'I'm sorry I was a bit ornery. Sometimes on your birthday, you get to think about things and you start to fret.' She paused. 'I like these people, you know. They don't know how weird they are, but then the whole country's a bit weird.'

Pom Pom nodded. 'Sometimes I sit and think how lucky I am to be where I am, and to be who I happen to be. And to be able to get on my bike and go where I like. And study courtly poetry. In Provençal. And to have tenure. What's not to like about that?'

'It's called good fortune,' said Alice. 'And each of us needs to think like that from time to time.'

Pom Pom looked thoughtful. 'We really are very lucky, aren't we? I have John back home, who's happy to look after the kids while I go off on study leave. He never complains.'

'You don't go that often,' said Alice. 'Every three years isn't much. And he has those fishing trips of his to Alaska.'

'Very cold, Alaska. I miss him, you know.'

'And I miss Eddie,' mused Alice. 'He's the ideal husband – no question about it. And, of course, I have great friends. You. Molly. Jean. All the girls in the bike club.'

'We're all very blessed,' said Pom Pom.

They ate their sandwiches. Then they lay back on the rug, each looking up at the sky above them, each lost in private thoughts, each in her individual but not dissimilar way content to have found happiness in a world that did not always hand out happiness to everybody who sought it.

Into the Closet

Von Igelfeld was enjoying that feeling of satisfaction that can come to those who know they have done the right thing. It is often short-lived, as it may be followed by thoughts of what one has missed, had one not been so susceptible to conscience and therefore done the wrong thing. In von Igelfeld's case there was no such remorse, as he had decided it would no longer be a hardship to wait to read Professor Fantozzi's chapter, particularly since he already knew that its tone was extremely complimentary. It is easier, he discovered, to put off the pleasure of reading an encomium than not to know precisely what is in an unfriendly review, for example. A pleasure postponed, he thought, is often all the sweeter for the wait.

By the time he got back to the Institute after the ill-fated visit to Herr Durchdenwald's office, he was in a thoroughly good mood. He had debated with himself whether he should tell Herr Huber that his recommendation had come to nothing. He did not want to hurt the Librarian's feelings – Herr

Huber always went out of his way to be helpful – but the fact of the matter was that he had made a thoroughly unsuitable suggestion and it was always possible that he might unwittingly cause difficulties by recommending Herr Durchdenwald to others.

He made his way to the library, where he found Herr Huber instructing young Herr Hühnerbein in some cataloguing task.

'I am showing Herr Hühnerbein how to deal with a particularly tricky issue of classification,' said Herr Huber, standing up from his task. 'We have a book here that is purportedly about Icelandic modal verbs. That's simple enough, of course, but the author expounds his theories about Sanskrit, and also wanders off into a discussion of Finno-Ugric subjunctives.'

Von Igelfeld shook his head in disapproval. 'That sort of thing is becoming far more common than it used to be,' he said. 'People should stick to the point.'

'It's because people like to let it all hang out,' ventured Herr Hühnerbein.

Both von Igelfeld and Herr Huber looked at him discouragingly.

'That's not very helpful, Herr Hühnerbein,' said Herr Huber. 'But thank you, anyway.'

Von Igelfeld indicated that he wanted to talk to Herr Huber in private, and the young librarian went off to perform some other task.

'He's a very competent young man,' said Herr Huber. 'I'm not sure that he'll ever make a head librarian, but certainly deputy librarian lies within his grasp – if he controls himself and stops using these slang expressions. I've spoken to him about it, but I'm not sure that he fully understands. He told me he was *cool* with what I said. I'm not sure what he meant by that.'

Von Igelfeld sighed. 'Sometimes these young people don't mean anything at all.' He paused. 'But that's not what I came to discuss with you, Herr Huber. I came to tell you that I went to see Herr Durchdenwald, as you suggested.'

'Ah yes,' said Herr Huber. 'And was he helpful?'

Von Igelfeld shook his head. 'No, it was a most unsuccessful visit.'

Herr Huber looked dismayed. 'What went wrong, Professor von Igelfeld? I would have thought it would be a simple matter.'

'Everything went wrong,' said von Igelfeld. 'He indicated that he would only help if I gave him something in return. And I refused.'

Herr Huber raised an eyebrow. 'Money?' he asked.

'No, he wanted me to do something to help his son to get a university place.'

Herr Huber was silent. Then he said, 'Are you sure about this, Professor von Igelfeld?'

Von Igelfeld made an impatient gesture. 'Of course I'm sure, Herr Huber.'

Herr Huber looked away. It seemed most unlikely to him that a politician of Herr Durchdenwald's standing would abuse his position in such a way. He looked back at von Igelfeld. 'He is a progressive politician, of course. You do know that his party is committed to progress?'

'I know that,' said von Igelfeld curtly.

'You don't think you might have misunderstood what he said to you?' Herr Huber pressed.

Von Igelfeld did not hesitate. 'Certainly not,' he snapped. 'He made himself abundantly clear.'

Herr Huber bit his lip. Was this further evidence of the crisis from which von Igelfeld was possibly suffering? Was this the paranoia one read about in the newspapers? He might have prolonged the discussion further, but he decided that it would be better to remain detached.

'I am very sorry to hear that you had that experience,' he said.

'And so am I, Herr Huber,' von Igelfeld retorted. 'I suggest that in future you are a bit more careful with your recommendations. This is not a criticism, I hasten to point out – it is merely an observation.'

Herr Huber nodded. Professor Unterholzer was probably right after all. They would all have to be very careful indeed.

Von Igelfeld looked at Herr Huber. Could he really have written that anonymous letter? Perhaps he had. But did it matter? He wondered whether he should raise the matter, but decided against it. Herr Huber meant well. That was the important thing. There was nothing threatening in the letter – merely a warning of a danger that did not really exist anyway. He would ignore the matter and only respond if he were to receive another anonymous letter from him. In that case he would write back to Herr Huber, anonymously of course, and suggest that he stop writing anonymous letters. He smiled to himself, pleased at the neatness of his solution.

Having delivered his rebuke to Herr Huber, von Igelfeld decided to return to his room. He was working on an article for the next issue of the *Zeitschrift*, and there were footnotes to be checked. It was not a task he enjoyed, but at least it was something to do that would keep his mind occupied. He knew that he was distracted – and he knew the reason why this was so. It was all to do with Pom Pom. She had unsettled him. It worried him that he seemed to be spending so much time thinking about her. Was she thinking about him too? He hoped she was.

To get from the library to his office at the other end of the building required him to pass first Prinzel's room, and then, a few doors further on, Unterholzer's. Prinzel's door was closed, but he could hear Prinzel within, engaged in what sounded like a telephone conversation.

'I'm going to pass this information on to Zimmermann,' Prinzel could be heard saying. 'It's exactly the sort of thing he would like to hear.'

Von Igelfeld resisted the temptation to linger, so that he might hear more of this conversation. Once one started listening in at the doors of others, it was but a short step to reading their mail. He would not begin that downhill path. And yet, what information was Prinzel planning to pass on to Zimmermann? Von Igelfeld knew that Prinzel had met Zimmermann, but he did not think he knew him all that well. If anybody should be in touch with the great scholar in Hamburg, then surely it should be he himself, von Igelfeld, rather than Prinzel or, *a fortiori*, Unterholzer. He would not listen in, but he might say something at coffee the following day. He might ask, innocently enough, whether anybody had recently heard from Zimmermann, and he would watch closely to see how Prinzel reacted. If he felt guilty – as was likely – then it would show in his demeanour: Prinzel was a man of complete probity and would never dissemble or tell an untruth.

He passed on. Now he was at Unterholzer's door, and he saw that it was slightly ajar. That was unusual: Unterholzer discouraged people from dropping in, and normally kept his door firmly shut when he was in the Institute.

He hesitated. There was no sound coming from within and, as he took a step forward, he found that he could see Unterholzer's desk from where he was standing in the corridor. And there was Unterholzer's chair, quite empty.

Looking over his shoulder to check that nobody was behind him in the corridor, he gave the door a slight push.

Into the Closet

It was enough to allow him to see that there was nobody in Unterholzer's office.

He felt his heart beating loud within his breast. Again, he looked over his shoulder. There was nobody about.

He thought: if Unterholzer didn't want anybody to see inside his office, then why would he leave his door ajar? Leaving it open was, in a way, an invitation to any passer-by to survey what was within. It was, perhaps, an endorsement of the open-plan approach to offices, under which everybody could see what was happening in the working place. Von Igelfeld had never agreed with that sort of thing, but it was quite possible that Unterholzer did.

And anyway, he told himself, it's not as if I am proposing to *remove* anything from Unterholzer's office – all that I want to do is . . .

And there it was, on Unterholzer's desk, in such a position that it could hardly be missed: Professor Fantozzi's book. There would be no harm – none at all – in having a quick look at the relevant chapter. He would not remove the book – that would be going too far – he would simply *inspect* it – as he had every right to do. It was Unterholzer who was in the wrong here: he was denying a colleague the right to consult a book that belonged to the Institute. His action was an offence against the spirit of co-operation that lay at the heart of what universities did. Unterholzer should be ashamed of himself.

His mind made up, von Igelfeld slipped into the office

and picked up the book that was lying alongside a pile of papers on Unterholzer's desk. He noticed, with some distaste, the disorder of the desk: while Prinzel and von Igelfeld were scrupulously neat, Unterholzer had always been somewhat disorganised. *Untidy desk*, thought von Igelfeld, *untidy mind* ... But this was not the time to worry about Unterholzer's personal habits – not with the copy of Giovanni Fantozzi's *Comparative Linguistic Observations* at last in his hands.

He opened the volume. Somebody, presumably Unterholzer himself, had inserted a folded piece of paper into the book to act as a bookmark. It was at this point that the book naturally fell open, and von Igelfeld caught his breath as he saw the exposed chapter heading. *Portuguese Irregular Verbs: a milestone in scholarship*. And there, at the head of the chapter, just as Professor Garelli-Ferrari had told him, von Igelfeld saw a photograph of himself receiving his honorary doctorate from the Gregorian University in Rome.

Rome ... The memory came back to him now of that triumphant day when the Rector of the University had called him to the stage in the University's hall at the base of the Quirinal Hill and delivered to the assembled company a tribute to his work. And here, under the photograph of that scene, was Fantozzi's sentence: *The author, with his typical modesty, receives one of his many distinctions.* Von Igelfeld trembled. How very generous of Professor Fantozzi – in a world where so many seemed to take more delight in diminishing people than in praising them. He would repay him; he would definitely return the compliment, perhaps in a future issue of the *Zeitschrift*, when he might refer to Fantozzi's work as 'groundbreaking' or 'magisterial'. There would be some way of reciprocating his generosity. It might even be possible to nominate Fantozzi for an honorary degree, although that would involve a certain amount of lobbying. Prinzel would support him, of course – he always did – and he would be able to make a special approach to His Magnificence the Rector, who had a reputation for fairness and approachability. He would show him this chapter – when he eventually was able to get his own copy of the book – and stress to him how much this Italian recognition meant to the reputation of the University of Regensburg.

Von Igelfeld began to read the chapter, which, in its laudatory tone, fully lived up to the promise of the title. But he had not gone much beyond the first page when he was disturbed by the sound of voices drifting down the corridor outside the room. It was Unterholzer, and, in the background, the equally recognisable voice of Herr Huber, and they were approaching the very office in which von Igelfeld was engaged in his unauthorised incursion.

For a few seconds, von Igelfeld froze. Then, hastily replacing the book on the desk, he looked about him for an escape route. He could not go out of the door through which he had entered, as that led straight into the corridor along which Unterholzer and Herr Huber were making their way.

He looked at the window. That was large enough to climb through, but the office was not on the ground floor and there was a considerable drop to the flowerbeds down below.

His eye fell on the large cupboard that occupied one corner of the room. Such cupboards were a feature of many of the offices in the building, and von Igelfeld himself had one. They had originally been installed so that professors would have somewhere to hang their academic gowns, but people used them for all sorts of other storage purposes. With any luck, Unterholzer's cupboard would not be so full as to make it impossible for von Igelfeld to hide within it. And when he quickly crossed the room and opened the cupboard door he discovered to his relief that this was the case: although there was an umbrella and a small suitcase that had to be shifted, there was ample room for von Igelfeld to conceal himself and pull the door to.

He did this just in time. From his dark hiding place, he heard the voices of Unterholzer and Herr Huber get closer and closer; then they were in the room and the office door was closed behind them.

Von Igelfeld heard everything, even if the voices of his two colleagues were slightly muffled by the cupboard door. To begin with, it was Herr Huber who was talking.

'... and she said, that is the man who was selling my wife the bread, that it had been baked that morning. But my wife has a nose for these things, and she said to him that it was at least two days old and that they shouldn't call it fresh

Into the Closet

bread if it had been baked the previous day. Don't you agree, Professor Unterholzer? Don't you think that's misleading?'

Unterholzer's reply came quickly. 'Your wife is quite right, Herr Huber. Frau Unterholzer also insists on absolutely fresh bread, but ... '

Herr Huber did not let him finish. 'I'm not saying that they can't sell it at all. That would be wasteful. All that I'm saying – or rather, that my wife was saying, is that descriptions should be accurate. That's not too much to ask, I think.'

Unterholzer now cleared his throat quite loudly. 'Very interesting, Herr Huber, but I wanted to talk to you about something confidential. Would you care to take a seat?'

Von Igelfeld heard a chair being drawn up.

'It's about our dear colleague, Professor von Igelfeld,' Unterholzer began. 'As you know, I am very concerned about him. I feel that there are signs that it's all becoming too stressful for him. I think that he may need a bit of help. A rest, perhaps. These days the University is very careful to ensure that its staff aren't subjected to too much strain. Poor Professor von Igelfeld has so much on his plate that perhaps he would benefit from a bit of help. A period of furlough, for example. Six months – perhaps even a year – away from the stresses and strains of what is, after all, a very demanding job.'

'Very demanding,' interjected Herr Huber. 'And we are under great pressure in the library too. We try to catalogue all new acquisitions within three weeks, but even with the best will in the world there are ... '

'Indeed,' Unterholzer interjected. 'But the point is this: will you be prepared to confirm the report that I intend to make to Herr Uber-Huber? Will you be able to back me up in my suggestion that poor Professor von Igelfeld is a candidate for sick leave?'

Herr Huber hesitated. He did not approve of Herr Uber-Huber; he did not like the pretentiousness of a Huber who tried to promote himself above other Hubers. And he was not absolutely certain that there was anything wrong with von Igelfeld – not so certain as to feel confident in making an official report to the University authorities.

Unterholzer sensed the Librarian's reservations. 'I imagine that you might need further evidence of Professor von Igelfeld's instability,' he said. 'I fully understand that. And I have a suggestion to make in that regard.'

Herr Huber waited.

'I have invited Professor von Igelfeld to dinner,' he said. 'Frau Unterholzer's cousin, Klaus-Peter, is a psychiatrist. We intend to invite him to dinner on the same evening, so he will have the chance to assess our dear afflicted colleague – without his knowing it, of course.'

Herr Huber looked doubtful.

'The ends justify the means, Herr Huber,' said Unterholzer. 'If we did nothing, imagine how guilty we would feel if Professor von Igelfeld became completely unstable. This is all in his best interests – without any shadow of doubt.'

Herr Huber still hesitated.

'And we shall invite our American visitors,' continued Unterholzer. 'The presence of Professor Pom Pom Boisseau is likely to bring out the sort of behaviour that will enable Klaus-Peter to make a diagnosis. She seems to be a precipitating factor, I think.'

Herr Huber sighed. Unterholzer was right: if they did nothing, and von Igelfeld's condition deteriorated, they would have a long time to regret it. Reluctantly he agreed.

'And I think it would be best if you came to the dinner too,' said Unterholzer. 'It will be useful to have you there if . . . if the worst happens.'

Herr Huber's eyes widened. What, he wondered, would the worst be? Would von Igelfeld be taken off in a straitjacket? Did they still use straitjackets, or would he simply be given a sedative and led meekly away? Both of these possibilities seemed deeply unattractive and were without precedent, he thought, in the entire history of the Institute. Not once, since the foundation of the Institute in 1897, had one of the senior professors been removed in such circumstances, and for that prospect then to face Professor Dr Dr (*honoris causa*) (*mult.*) Moritz-Maria von Igelfeld seemed unthinkable. And yet the unthinkable, as every historian knew, happened from time to time, as if to remind us, should we need a reminder, that the affairs of men were ultimately subject to the whims of fate; were as unpredictable as the weather; were quite indifferent to justice and desert.

Inside his cupboard, von Igelfeld listened with growing indignation. It was clear to him that of the two plotters, Unterholzer was undoubtedly the most perfidious. Herr Huber was easily led – everybody was aware of that – and his involvement in this plot anyway seemed to be very much one of the junior party. He could be discounted, even forgiven, whereas Unterholzer would in due course have to bear full responsibility for the whole shocking web of intrigue. For a few moments, von Igelfeld considered bursting out from the cupboard and confronting Unterholzer, but then he realised that he would have to give some explanation for his presence in the cupboard, and try as he might he could think of none that was in the slightest bit credible. No, he would remain hidden and attend Unterholzer's dinner without giving any indication that he knew of his colleague's ulterior motive.

In the office, Herr Huber now rose to his feet. He had to get back to the library, he said, where there was outstanding cataloguing to be done. For his part, Unterholzer announced that he would be leaving too, as he had to call in at a delicatessen to collect an order that Frau Unterholzer had placed by phone. Hearing this, von Igelfeld felt a surge of relief. It had crossed his mind that Unterholzer might settle down in his office for the remainder of the day, and that remaining concealed in the cupboard would be an uncomfortable ordeal. Fortunately, that was not to happen.

He heard Herr Huber leave the room, and then came the sound of Unterholzer pushing his chair back. Then there were footsteps, and for a dreadful moment he thought they were approaching the cupboard. They passed by, though, and the next thing that von Igelfeld heard was the opening of the door that Herr Huber had closed behind him when they had entered. Then the door was closed once again and there came the sound, just discernible, of the two conspirators retreating down the corridor. Von Igelfeld let those die away completely before he tentatively opened his cupboard door and peered out into the room. Seeing that all danger was over, he made his way rapidly out of Unterholzer's office, pausing only to note that the offending copy of Professor Fantozzi's book had been removed from the desk and was nowhere to be seen.

Oysters Rockefeller

The Institute's coffee room was one of the smaller rooms in the building, and yet it was, in many respects, the most significant. It was here that the academic staff, and by historical custom Herr Huber, who was, strictly speaking, an ancillary, non-academic member of the University community, met each morning for the purposes of drinking coffee and dealing with matters of importance. As one might expect of any common room, it was a clearing house of information – the parish pump, so to speak, around which village news was shared and dissected. And like all such institutions, it was set about with issues and potential pitfalls for the unwary.

Without doubt, the most contentious issue relating to the coffee room was the question of who was entitled to use it. Over the years, this had given rise to difficulties every bit as complex as those surrounding the famous Schleswig–Holstein question, that immensely convoluted dispute as to the ownership of the duchies of Schleswig and Holstein, to which Denmark and the German confederation both laid claim during the nineteenth century. That long-running issue had prompted Lord Palmerston, the British Foreign Secretary, to utter his famous observation: 'Only three people have really understood the Schleswig–Holstein business: the Prince Consort, who is dead; a German professor, who has gone mad; and I, who have forgotten all about it.'

The tides of argument and uncertainty that washed at the shores of the coffee room were caused by the fact that it had only seven chairs. There had been talk of installing a bench-seat underneath the window that would have provided seating for an additional three people, although that in itself was the subject of heated debate, with von Igelfeld insisting that were such a seat to be added, it could only accommodate two people if either of them happened to be larger in the beam than normal. This had resulted in an awkward exchange as to what was meant by normal. That discussion was dominated by von Igelfeld and Prinzel, both of whom, although tall, were relatively slender at the waist. Unterholzer, by contrast, was every bit as tall as Prinzel, even if slightly shorter than von Igelfeld, and yet, as the eye travelled down his figure, it could hardly be unaware of a spreading out, not unlike the widening that occurs at the Nile or Mississippi Delta. If the two people who chose to sit on this hypothetical window seat were to be similar in shape to Unterholzer, then there would certainly be no room for a third. Von Igelfeld was on the verge of pointing that out, when he realised that Unterholzer might regard it as a tactless, not to say tasteless observation, and he did not use this obvious example to illustrate his point. As it happened, Prinzel was thinking exactly the same thing, although he came closer to articulating his thoughts than did von Igelfeld.

'It all depends on the size of the people who would wish to sit on this new seat,' he said. 'If they were the same shape as Un ... ' He stopped just in time. 'The same shape, that is, as some people one sees in the street these days, namely, a little bit on the large size, then only two such persons would be able to sit comfortably. That is, of course, an entirely theoretical observation and not intended to refer to anybody in particular.'

Unterholzer had looked at Prinzel suspiciously, but had said nothing, and the moment passed. No action was taken on the matter, and the possibility of creating a window seat was never again mentioned. The number of seats remained at seven, which meant that on normal days only four of them were occupied by the three professors, by academic entitlement, and by Herr Huber, in his capacity as librarian. That left three seats for visitors – although not every visitor was entitled to use the coffee room and to sit in one of these seats.

The position of visitors had been discussed at length over the years. An initial distinction was made between visitors from within the University and those from without. Internal visitors would be invited into the coffee room provided they were of sufficient seniority. This had been interpreted by von Igelfeld in such a way that meant that full professors from other departments would be admitted to the coffee room if official business brought them to the Institute. The position of those who were in the Institute other than on official business was unresolved. Von Igelfeld suggested that if they were not there in the course of their duties, then they had no business being in the Institute and were not entitled to avail themselves of the coffee room's facilities.

'We can't have just anybody coming from elsewhere in the University and drinking our coffee,' he said when the matter came up for discussion. 'The University of Regensburg is a large institution, and we can't provide hospitality for all its professors. Where would it end? What if people decided that they liked the atmosphere of our coffee room and started coming here from all sorts of departments. We'd get chemists and people traipsing in and drinking coffee. Would we have to charge them? What if a whole group of chemistry professors came in and took all or most of the chairs? Where would we go then?'

Herr Huber had agreed. 'A very similar issue arose in my aunt's nursing home,' he volunteered. 'They have a room for the nurses to take their coffee. There are people who bring supplies to the home – creams and things like that. They use these creams for dry skin, you see, because some of the residents have a real problem with that. Your skin gets drier when you get older, you know. My aunt has never had that problem, though. She's had wonderful skin all her life. And these people saw the nurses' coffee room and thought they were entitled to go in there because they had just delivered all those moisturising supplies. I suppose you can see it from their point of view. They've just brought all the creams and ...'

Unterholzer had cut him short. 'Very interesting, Herr Huber, but our problem is unlikely to be delivery men. They clearly have no claim to anything. Our problem will be with people from the University administration – accounts people and so on – who may find themselves here and see the coffee room ...'

'Or smell it,' interjected Herr Huber. 'You can smell the coffee as you walk down the corridor. Many people find that very inviting.'

Unterholzer ignored this. 'Or general administrators – what about them, I ask myself? What about that Herr Uber-Huber who keeps sticking his nose into other people's business? What about him? Do we want to come in here one morning and find him sitting in one of our chairs, telling us how to run our Institute? No thank you, is what I say to that.'

This brought a general chorus of agreement.

'He is to be discouraged in every way,' said von Igelfeld. 'I am not suggesting that we are rude to him – that would be to sink to his level. But we can ignore him. If nobody speaks to him, then he might be less inclined to send us circulars and so on.'

'These people are very thick-skinned,' said Prinzel. 'They often don't notice if people aren't speaking to them. They're so used to speaking *at* people that they just don't hear what anybody else is saying.'

Von Igelfeld expressed the view that this was very true. 'They're extremely self-centred,' he said. 'I suppose they are just one of the crosses it is our lot to bear.'

Such discussions were irregular, although they did occur even after the issues appeared to have been decided. What helped, though, was the preparation by von Igelfeld of a diagram, a map in essence, that showed the seven chairs and made it clear who sat where. On this map, von Igelfeld inscribed the names of the four regulars on their individual chairs – they always sat in the same place – and then labelled each of the remaining chairs 1, 2 and 3, in descending order of desirability. These were the visitor chairs, chair 1 being the most comfortable and best positioned, sited next to von Igelfeld's own seat; chair 2 being next to Prinzel; and chair 3 being beside Herr Huber, but with Unterholzer on the other side. The piece of paper on which this information was recorded was laminated by one of the secretaries, and although it was not actually pinned on the noticeboard, it was readily available as an *aide-mémoire* in a drawer under the shelf on which the cups and saucers were kept.

Oysters Rockefeller

On the morning following von Igelfeld's incursion into Unterholzer's office, there was only one chair left unoccupied at morning coffee, as Pom Pom and Alice had both joined their hosts and had been allocated chairs 1 and 2 respectively. They were not regular attendees of the morning coffee session, as Pom Pom had discovered a coffee bar nearby that was frequented by members of the motorcycling community, and they tended to prefer going there. On this occasion, though, Unterholzer had specifically asked them to attend, his intention being to issue the invitation to dinner that would include them. If he were to invite the Americans publicly in that way, then he thought that von Igelfeld would be unlikely to feel suspicious.

Von Igelfeld, of course, was delighted to find Pom Pom already there when he arrived in the coffee room, and to see, moreover, that Prinzel had guided her to her proper seat.

'What a pleasant surprise,' he said, bowing slightly in her direction and then doing the same towards Alice. 'I take it that everything is working out well?'

'You bet,' said Pom Pom. 'We're making great progress with our project.'

'Yes,' agreed Alice. 'Everything's hunky-dory.'

Herr Huber asked them whether they were finding the library resources adequate. 'We certainly are,' Pom Pom said. 'This is a wonderful collection you have here.'

'That is thanks to Herr Huber,' Prinzel said. 'He sees everything.'

Herr Huber lowered his head in acknowledgement of the compliment.

'Even books by lesser-known Italian scholars,' said von Igelfeld, giving Unterholzer a sideways glance as he spoke.

Unterholzer said nothing, but reached forward for his cup of coffee.

'Although,' von Igelfeld continued, 'there can be a surprising demand even for those. That is why it's important not to hold on to library books for too long. We must give others a chance to read the things they need to read.'

'Quite right,' said Pom Pom, who was, of course, ignorant of the subtext to these particular comments. 'There's nothing worse than having to wait for weeks and you know all along that somebody else is just hogging a book. That happened back home once. We had an inconsiderate colleague who sat on a book that Alice was desperate to consult. He knew that she wanted it, but he held on to it until the very day on which the loan expired. Can you believe it?'

If von Igelfeld had scripted this intervention, he could not have come up with a weightier reproach to Unterholzer. Now he nodded his agreement sagely, only glancing briefly at Unterholzer to see his reaction. Unterholzer had a skin as thick as that of a rhinoceros – everybody knew that, thought von Igelfeld, and he appeared indifferent to Pom Pom's comment. So, von Igelfeld confined himself to saying 'Well, really!' and left it at that.

Oysters Rockefeller

Unterholzer now broached the subject of the dinner party. 'Frau Unterholzer and I would like to invite everybody to dinner,' he announced. 'It's some time since we had a dinner party, and we think it would be very pleasant to get everybody together.'

'Oh my,' said Pom Pom. 'How very kind.'

'Lovely,' said Alice.

Von Igelfeld smiled benignly. 'What a nice gesture, Professor Unterholzer,' he said.

'Even me?' asked Herr Huber.

'Of course,' said Unterholzer. He had told Herr Huber yesterday that he would be included, but he could hardly remind him now of the earlier invitation.

Unterholzer told everybody about the date that had been settled upon – the dinner was to be in three days' time, on a Friday evening. He then asked if there were any dietary requirements – a question that elicited a response from nobody, apart from Herr Huber, who announced that much as he liked the taste of oysters, he found that they disagreed with him. 'I'm told this is a common complaint,' he said. 'A lot of people find that oysters make them ill.'

'It's a good thing you told us about that, Herr Huber,' said Pom Pom. 'If you came to see us down in New Orleans we might have taken you to one of our seafood places for Oysters Rockefeller. They were invented down there.'

'In a famous restaurant called Antoine's,' said Alice. 'Back at the end of the nineteenth century. The place was owned by a man called Jules Alciatore. He called them Oysters Rockefeller because the sauce was so rich.'

Von Igelfeld looked fondly at Pom Pom. He liked the openness, the generosity of the Americans. Here they were inviting Herr Huber to visit New Orleans when nobody would ever have invited him to go anywhere. He smiled at her, and to his complete delight, she smiled back.

'And you, Moritz-Maria,' Pom Pom said. 'You must come down to see us. We'd show you the Quarter.'

'I would enjoy that very much,' said von Igelfeld. 'And the Bayou.'

'That too,' said Pom Pom.

'And might it be possible,' von Igelfeld continued, 'to meet your colleague who is working on communication among oysters? I was most intrigued when I heard about that project.'

Pom Pom nodded. 'If he's around, there'd be no problem with that. He spends a lot of time working at sea. But he comes ashore most weekends.'

'When would be convenient for me to travel to New Orleans?' asked von Igelfeld.

Pom Pom glanced at Alice. 'Some time in the future,' she said. 'We'd have to look at diaries.'

'I can fetch mine,' said von Igelfeld.

'I need to discuss things with our Dean,' said Pom Pom quickly. 'We'll get back to you on that one.'

Unterholzer felt embarrassed on von Igelfeld's behalf. You

would think he would know that English-speaking people, unlike the Germans, rarely meant what they said. Both the Americans and the British invited people to drop in to see them, but never really meant it. Von Igelfeld was just far too literal – he should have known that.

With everybody dispersed after morning coffee, von Igelfeld returned to his room, dallying on his way, as he was in no mood to hurry. He felt strangely unmoved by the prospect of Unterholzer's dinner party and by the fact that one of the guests would be a psychiatrist, whose sole objective would be to assess his sanity. There was nothing at all wrong with him, and the prospect of several hours under psychiatric observation did not overly concern him. In fact, he was rather looking forward to it, as, forewarned of what lay ahead, he might even be able to confuse and subvert Unterholzer's plan. It would be a pleasure, in fact, to confound their machinations and at the same time take advantage of this opportunity to spend a bit more social time with Pom Pom. He would have a discreet word with Frau Unterholzer, he thought, and ask whether he could possibly be seated next to her psychiatric in-law, so as to allow for intimate conversation without alerting the rest of the table as to what was going on. He could also ask Frau Unterholzer if she could place Pom Pom on his other side, so that he might deepen his blossoming friendship with the distinguished American scholar. Unlike her calculating husband, Frau Unterholzer was obliging, and he was sure that she would readily accede to his request.

He smiled to himself. He rather enjoyed being in love, if that was the state in which he currently felt himself. It must be, he thought: why else would he feel this delicious sensation of exhilaration, in which the world, and all its incidentals, seemed touched with a golden light of possibility and affection. So, this was what love was all about. So, this was what the great poets felt when they wrote odes to their lovers. It was a delightful feeling, von Igelfeld decided – and one that he believed would become more and more consuming the closer he came to Pom Pom. *Pom Pom* – what an entirely suitable name. There was something light and ethereal about it. He smiled, as, for a moment, he envisaged a biker Pom Pom on a heavenly motorbike, wings swept back by the wind, tracing an arc across the sky, engaged in some celestial mission. That was what the world needed, he thought: powers for good that were somehow more convincing, more *decisive*.

An Evening with the *Korps*

On one of the days before the Unterholzer dinner party, von Igelfeld was obliged to attend a social function to which he was looking forward with much less enthusiasm than he felt at the prospect of dinner in the company of Pom Pom and Alice, and particularly of Pom Pom. This function was a meeting of a student *Korps*, to be held in a beerhall outside the city. Von Igelfeld would never normally consider going anywhere near a beerhall, nor would he willingly attend any student function, but on this occasion he found himself obliged to accept the invitation.

That had come from a twenty-year-old student of architecture, Friedrich Baumgarten-Wolf, who was the stepson of a distant von Igelfeld cousin, Karl-Heinz von Tiefenhausen. It was some years since von Igelfeld had been in the company of Karl-Heinz, whom he met from time to time at extended family occasions, and he barely remembered his wife, who ran an atelier in which she made elaborate hats. Karl-Heinz owned a string of riding stables as well as a factory that made stainless-steel fittings for yachts. He seemed proud of von Igelfeld's eminence, and had even bought a copy of *Portuguese Irregular Verbs* when it was first published, although von Igelfeld doubted that he had ever read it.

When young Friedrich first arrived in Regensburg to study for a degree in architecture, his father had written to inform von Igelfeld that his stepson would shortly be enrolling at the University and asked him whether he could keep an eye on him. 'He's a very agreeable young man,' he wrote, 'and I imagine that he will be diligent in his architectural studies. He has, however, a tendency to fall in with rather fast company, and I would be most grateful if you would let me know from time to time how he's doing. He's never been a great letter-writer and his mother despairs of ever hearing from him during termtime. He also spends money rather freely, but I suppose the young do that because they haven't had to *make* the money they spend. And he needs to watch how much he drinks, incidentally – but students are like that, of course. He should be no trouble, though.'

Von Igelfeld had met Friedrich, who asked to be called Freddie, a few weeks after the young man first came to Regensburg. He had written him a note, suggesting that he call in at the Institute, provided he could find the time to be away from his studies. 'I imagine you are very busy,' von Igelfeld had written. 'But it is important to have at least some time away from your books.' Freddie had telephoned to say that he could come to see von Igelfeld at any time, and that very afternoon, in fact, would be highly suitable.

They had met in von Igelfeld's office, and the meeting, von Igelfeld thought, had gone rather well. Freddie was a personable young man, with a pleasing, open expression and a wide smile. He was athletic in his build and von Igelfeld found that he reminded him, more than of anybody else, of Florianus Prinzel in his student days. Prinzel had been a great sportsman, the winner of numerous running trophies, and had been admired for this prowess by von Igelfeld, who had never had any sporting talent. Prinzel, like Freddie, had also been a member of a student *Korps* and had been involved in a duel in which the top of his nose had been sliced off. Von Igelfeld had witnessed this unfortunate incident, and although the nose had been repaired, the doctor had been drunk, with the result that the detached scrap of tissue had been sewn back on upside down. It was not a big thing, in time becoming barely noticeable, but it had left von Igelfeld with a distrust of student *Korps* and their dangerous habits.

Von Igelfeld's first meeting with Freddie had gone well, and just before he left the young man had been emboldened to raise a potentially awkward issue with this distant stepcousin of his.

'It's very expensive being a student,' he said to von Igelfeld. 'There are all these books to buy. And the *Mensa*, of course, is not as cheap as it used to be. A very simple meal these days can cost five euros – and that's without beer.'

Von Igelfeld sympathised. 'The cost of living is always rising,' he said. 'I have never heard of it going down.'

'And then there are all the other costs,' Freddie continued. 'Clothing. Shaving cream. One's phone contract. Paper. Bus fares. You name it – it's costing more and more.'

'The Government needs to do something about it,' said von Igelfeld. 'That's what they're for, I believe.' He thought of Herr Durchdenwald: he was part of the Government – was he doing anything about the cost of living? He looked at Freddie, who did not seem in the slightest bit undernourished. Nor did his clothes look cheap: they were well cut and made of what must have been expensive cloth. That was what one would expect, he said to himself, of a member of the von Tiefenhausen family. Karl-Heinz von Tiefenhausen would be a wealthy man, von Igelfeld imagined, and would certainly be in a position to give his stepson a generous allowance.

Freddie assumed an apologetic expression. 'I'm currently a bit short,' he said, his voice lowered as he imparted the confidence. 'My landlord is threatening to throw me out unless I pay the rent by next Friday. Imagine it. Out in the street. Just like that.'

Von Igelfeld frowned. 'But you get an allowance from your stepfather, I assume.'

'Oh yes,' said Freddie. 'Father is generous enough, bless his cotton socks. It's just that he doesn't understand how expensive things are these days. He lives in a bit of a bubble, I'm afraid.'

'Could you not ask him for an advance?' asked von Igelfeld.

Freddie shook his head. 'Father's heart is very weak,' he said. 'The slightest thing can upset him very badly, and then his angina gets going. We have to be very careful, I can tell you. If I told him that I needed an advance on my allowance, his blood pressure would go through the roof. We could lose him – just like that.' Freddie snapped his fingers before continuing, 'Just like that. Poof! Gone!'

Von Igelfeld was not sure what to say.

'Which is why I wondered whether you might let me have a couple of hundred,' said Freddie. 'Say, four hundred, to be on the safe side. Five, maybe.'

Von Igelfeld stared at him. This was quite unexpected, and he would normally have summarily dismissed any request for money from a student, but this was not just any student – this was one who was vaguely related – a sort of step-von Igelfeld, and that made it hard to refuse.

Five hundred euros changed hands, and Freddie was effusive in his expression of gratitude. 'It's very kind of you to give me this, Cousin Moritz-Maria,' he said. 'I shan't forget this.'

Nothing was said about the money being a loan, and no offer was ever made to repay it. But it was clear to von Igelfeld that Freddie was grateful, and it was this gratitude that led to the invitation that von Igelfeld eventually received to accompany the young man to a special meeting of his *Korps*.

The Lost Language of Oysters

'We are occasionally allowed to take a guest to one of these evenings,' he said. 'And I thought that you might enjoy it, Herr Cousin, you being a bit old-fashioned ... I mean traditional in your outlook.'

Von Igelfeld had accepted out of duty, and now the night of the *Korps* meeting had arrived and he was waiting for Freddie to pick him up in a taxi that would take them both to the beerhall where the members were to assemble.

'It will be a very good evening,' Freddie said, as they set off. 'You will meet my friends, Willy and Felix. You'll like Felix – he's a very fine boxer – middleweight. His father has a private plane – a six-seater, even – and has offered to fly us to the Czech Republic for a beer festival next month.'

'I see,' said von Igelfeld.

'Willy plays the trombone in a marching band,' Freddie continued. 'His girlfriend is a singer in a nightclub. She's Belarusian, but she prefers to live in Germany. Who wouldn't? You should see her – actually you probably shouldn't! She supports Willy with the tips that the nightclub customers give her. Apparently they're very generous. We're talking hundreds. Real money.'

'Friends are important,' said von Igelfeld.

'Sure,' said Freddie. 'Friends, beer, girls – three essentials for the balanced life. Plato said that, I believe. Only joking, Cousin Moritz-Maria! Your stuff's important, too – all that stuff you do.'

They arrived at the beerhall. There was a notice prominently displayed outside reading *Private Function* and various young men were milling about at the front door. They were wearing, von Igelfeld noticed, peaked caps of the sort traditionally sported by conductors on trains. There was a small badge at the front, and round the cap itself was a band of red and blue piping.

'That's our cap,' said Freddie. 'The red represents blood and the blue represents the tradition that binds us all together.'

'Very interesting,' said von Igelfeld. 'Tradition is so important. These people who say that tradition is meaningless . . .' He paused. 'What blood?'

Freddie did not answer. 'Traditions like this are harmless. If we want to dress up in caps and so on, what harm are we doing to anybody else? That's what I'd like to know.'

They went inside. At the door, a muscular young man wearing an academic gown listened to Freddie's explanation that this was his guest, his stepfather's cousin, Professor Dr Dr Moritz-Maria von Igelfeld.

The young man was impressed. 'This is a great honour, Professor,' he said. 'The *Korps* has not had a visit from the professoriate for a long time. It's so good to see you.' He paused. 'I imagine it will remind you of your own student days, even if those were a very long time ago.'

Von Igelfeld said nothing, but inclined his head slightly in acknowledgment, and they went inside.

There were at least one hundred young men inside the

beerhall, all wearing the *Korps* cap. A number of members, lined up on a stage, had begun to sing, receiving boisterous encouragement from their fellows in the body of the hall. Von Igelfeld recognised the song – and felt a pang of regret as he heard its words: *O alte Burschenherrlichkeit*. The chorus was taken up by the those down below, who raised tankards of beer as they sang. And then, as the last notes of the *Burschenherrlichkeit* died away, the singers on the stage started the *Gaudeamus*. Von Igelfeld felt a lump in his throat: this was the song that he himself had sung, with Florianus Prinzel by his side, all these years ago. *Floreat Academia, floreant professores* . . . How could one be indifferent to such sentiments, expressed by generation upon generation of students, all the way back to the days invoked so powerfully by the *Carmina Burana*? He joined in, the words coming naturally to him because they had never really gone away.

A young man, wearing a blue jacket over which a sash of red had been draped, brought him a tall glass of beer and raised his own glass in a toast. Von Igelfeld took the glass, replied to the toast, and took a deep draught of beer. He was not normally a beer drinker, but this was refreshing and thirst-quenching. Another glass was soon produced, and the young man who had brought him the beer began to tell him about how he was studying medicine and hoped in due course to become a surgeon.

After the second beer, von Igelfeld had begun to enjoy himself. He had now had several conversations with other

An Evening with the Korps

members of the *Korps*, all of whom had been courteous and attentive. 'We don't get many professors coming to our meetings,' said one of them. 'I can't understand why.'

'Indeed,' said von Igelfeld, draining his glass. 'These are very civil occasions, I think.'

Von Igelfeld became aware that from one end of the hall there was emanating a series of shouts and cheers. Eager to find out what was happening, he made his way in that direction, to find himself standing in a crowd surrounding a cleared circle. In the circle, three pairs of young men were facing one another with drawn swords, their left arms raised in the classic *en garde* position of the fencer.

Von Igelfeld gasped. He had imagined that duelling had long since been abandoned by the young men who belonged to these clubs, but here they were facing up to one another with swords that were real and, by the look of things, razor-sharp.

There was a sudden clash of steel, followed by silence, and then by a cheer from the crowd. Two of the participants lowered their swords, which were taken over by other young men. There were cries and cheers, and another brief engagement took place.

Suddenly von Igelfeld felt himself being propelled forward.

'What about the Professor?' shouted a voice from the crowd.

'Yes, Herr Professor, Herr Professor!' chanted a group of young men at the front.

And then, before he knew what was happening, von Igelfeld had a sword thrust into his hand and he was pushed forward to face an opponent directly before him. This young man lowered his sword and then lifted it so that he could kiss the hilt in salute. Then, with a sudden swing, so rapid as to be almost invisible to the eye, the blade sliced through the air.

Von Igelfeld had no time to react. The next thing he felt was a sharp sensation on his right cheek, as if a bee or a horsefly had stung him. He reached up and touched his face. His fingers felt sticky and he looked down at them, at the bright red that had appeared on the tips.

'Oh, well done,' shouted one of the *Korps* members. He then moved forward and dabbed solicitously at von Igelfeld's cheek.

'Just a tiny nick,' he said. 'Nothing more than you might get while shaving. But congratulations nonetheless.'

The medical student to whom von Igelfeld had been talking earlier on now stepped forward and applied a small sticking plaster to von Igelfeld's cheek. 'That's very minor,' he said. 'You probably won't even get a scar, or, if you do, it will be a small one.'

Von Igelfeld was feeling slightly queasy – whether from overexcitement or from the consumption of three large glasses of beer. He had had a surfeit of this *Korps* occasion and wanted to get home. Searching the crowd, he eventually came across Freddie, who had missed the duel, but who

An Evening with the Korps

expressed admiration for the small wound now concealed behind the sticking plaster.

'You're really lucky to get that, Cousin Moritz-Maria,' he said. 'A lot of these *Kerle* would love to have something like that.' He paused. 'I hope you've enjoyed yourself.'

Von Igelfeld smiled. 'It has been very interesting,' he said. He felt a certain satisfaction at the turn of events. To have a duelling scar was a definite cachet in certain circles, and even if his was going to be very small, it would still give Herr Huber and Unterholzer something to think about. They would never be able to get a duelling scar because he could never imagine them attending one of these *Korps* meetings. A badge of honour required some sort of commitment – courage, even – and it seemed to von Igelfeld that these were qualities that were perhaps in short supply in the world of people like Unterholzer and Herr Huber. Pom Pom could not fail to be impressed, he told himself – and the thought made him feel pleasantly warm.

He said goodbye to Freddie, who promised to visit him shortly, and who would bring with him, he said, his friends Willy and Felix. Then, still feeling the effects of the beer – and the duel – he made his way outside and summoned a taxi to take him home.

In the rear-view mirror of the taxi, the driver glanced at von Igelfeld. He noticed the sticking plaster on his cheek. 'You people,' he said, shaking his head in disbelief. 'You'd think you'd know better, you really would.' And added, 'At your age, too.'

Von Igelfeld opened his mouth to protest, but closed it again without a word. There was no point in engaging with taxi drivers. With skills so sharp that they might have been honed in an ancient Greek academy of rhetoric, they always won.

White Shoes – and a Disclosure

Professors Pom Pom Boisseau and Alice Martinique were the first to arrive at the Unterholzer dinner party, ringing the doorbell at seven-thirty, a good fifteen minutes before the next guest.

As they waited for a response, Pom Pom observed to Alice, 'These people like promptness, it seems.'

Alice was not so sure. 'Maybe not in everything. Sometimes hosts need time to get things ready. You never know.'

'Possibly,' said Pom Pom. 'Local etiquette is a minefield. We forget that other people don't care about when you wear white shoes – unlike us.'

Alice laughed.

'White shoes? Bah!'

Pom Pom thought: you can say *bah*, but that's too easy. You can't get rid of the white shoes issue just by saying bah. Now she remembered how, as a girl, she had visited her aunts in Mobile, Alabama, and they had drummed it into her that white shoes could only be worn before Labor Day.

'White shoes,' said Pom Pom, dreamily.

Alice frowned. Did anybody still believe that? 'Do you still pay attention to that, Pommy?'

'Not me,' Pom Pom replied. 'But there might be some, you know. Beliefs don't just go away. There'll be people who still believe in that one. Country-club types, perhaps.'

'You know that they think it rude here to leave food on your plate,' said Alice. 'And no elbows on the table. Strictly *verboten*.'

'Oh my,' said Pom Pom. 'The things one has to remember. Do you think they have a *Fräulein Höflichkeit* – their Miss Manners?'

Alice did not have time to answer, as the door was now opened by Unterholzer, who smiled warmly and gave a slight bow of the head.

'I hope we're not early,' said Pom Pom.

Unterholzer was quick to reassure them. 'Perfect timing.'

He glanced over Pom Pom's shoulder into the street outside. 'No motorbikes?'

Pom Pom gave a playful laugh. 'We weren't sure about going to a dinner party in our leathers.'

'Perfectly acceptable,' said Unterholzer lightly. 'These days, anything goes.'

Frau Unterholzer now appeared from a door at the other end of the hall, and introductions were made. And at this

White Shoes – and a Disclosure

point, Walter, the Unterholzer dachshund, strapped into his supportive three-wheeled carriage, propelled himself into the room, gazing mournfully at the two visitors.

'My,' exclaimed Alice. 'There's a sight.'

'That's our Walter,' explained Frau Unterholzer. 'There's a story behind his . . . '

She did not finish, as the bell now rang and Unterholzer turned round to open the door. This time it was von Igelfeld, bearing a bunch of flowers.

'Ah, Professor von Igelfeld,' said Unterholzer. 'Here we are. Our two dear American visitors have just arrived.'

'So I see,' said von Igelfeld curtly, handing the flowers to Frau Unterholzer. She received them graciously. As she did so, von Igelfeld gave a broad smile in Pom Pom's direction.

But Pom Pom was paying attention to Walter, who was now tentatively licking her shoe. 'Such a friendly little fellow,' she said. And then, looking up, she continued, 'Frau Unterholzer was just about to tell us the story.'

Frau Unterholzer shot an anxious glance at her husband, who suddenly seemed to freeze.

'Maybe some other time,' he stuttered.

Von Igelfeld glanced down at Walter, and then quickly looked away again. The dog's plight was, in the view of some, *his* fault. Had he not, for complicated reasons, been pretending to be a professor of veterinary medicine, the student who carried out the amputation of three of

Walter's legs would not have done so – or would only have removed the one that needed such treatment. It was all so embarrassing.

'Yes, it has been a very warm day,' said Frau Unterholzer inconsequentially.

Unterholzer seized the opportunity. 'Yes, absolutely,' he said. 'Very warm.'

Alice was bending down to pat Walter's head. 'He must be a plucky little thing,' she said. 'Was he born this way?'

'I knew some folks who had a dog born short of a leg,' said Pom Pom. 'It was congenital. He got by just fine. But this little man seems to be missing ... how many is it? Three?'

Unterholzer was staring accusingly at von Igelfeld. Now he said, 'These things happen.'

'An accident?' asked Alice, as she straightened up from patting Walter.

Von Igelfeld said, 'I hope these flowers are ... '

He did not finish, as once again the doorbell sounded. This time it was Herr Huber, accompanied by Frau Huber.

'There's Walter,' exclaimed the Librarian, adding, 'with his wheels. They can do so much for dogs now, can't they?'

'Poor Walter,' said Frau Huber. 'I've always thought of him as being the bravest dog I know.'

'What happened?' asked Alice.

Unterholzer looked at his watch. 'We can't all stay here. Let's go into the living room and I shall get everyone

White Shoes – and a Disclosure

something to drink. My wife's cousin will be joining us, but he told us that he might be a bit late.'

'Duties at the hospital?' asked Herr Huber.

Unterholzer gave Herr Huber a discouraging glance. Von Igelfeld noticed this. 'Oh, yes?' he said brightly. 'What sort of doctor is your cousin, Frau Unterholzer?'

It was Unterholzer who replied. 'A very good one.' He looked relieved at having dodged the question so neatly.

Frau Unterholzer smiled. 'That goes without saying, I think.'

'But what does he specialise in?' pressed von Igelfeld. He knew, of course – but were they going to reveal it?

'He deals with . . . ' Unterholzer hesitated. 'With . . . medical matters.'

'He's a psychiatrist,' said Frau Unterholzer.

Von Igelfeld glanced at Frau Unterholzer. *She was not part of the conspiracy* – that much was apparent now.

'A psychiatrist?' said von Igelfeld, feigning surprise. And then, with a smile, 'We shall all have to be careful what we say, Herr Unterholzer, would you not agree?'

Alice laughed. 'Psychiatrists aren't like that. They don't go round trying to analyse people they meet.'

'Really?' said von Igelfeld. 'That's good to know. It could be quite unsettling if one thought that a psychiatrist was paying unwanted attention to one. Not, of course, that anybody would ever *ask* a psychiatrist to do such an unethical thing, would they?'

The question seemed to have been addressed to Unterholzer, and now all eyes turned to him. He gave an insouciant wave of his hand. 'Of course not,' he said airily. 'But let us progress to the living room, because otherwise we shall all still be standing here when it is time to go home.'

'That would be crazy,' joked Alice.

Pom Pom burst out laughing. 'Yes, crazy,' she said, adding, 'Of course.'

Cousin Klaus-Peter was a thin, elegantly dressed man in his late forties. He had slicked-back dark hair and spoke in slow, carefully constructed sentences, delivered with a slight lisp. There was something enigmatic about his manner, thought von Igelfeld: it was as if he knew something that others did not know, but that he would be unlikely to disclose.

Unterholzer introduced him to his guests. 'This is my wife's cousin,' he said. 'Dr Klaus-Peter Schröger.'

Dr Schröger shook hands with everybody in a formal manner, although when it came to Frau Unterholzer he embraced her, patting her gently on the shoulder while saying, 'There, there.' It was a curious thing to say, von Igelfeld felt – it sounded as if he was consoling her in some way. But for what? For being married to Unterholzer, perhaps, because that could hardly be easy, in all the circumstances. And to

White Shoes – and a Disclosure

have a disabled dog into the bargain, whose needs must at times be somewhat demanding; that was a small thing, perhaps, but small things could mount up and eventually make life very difficult

On being introduced to Pom Pom, Dr Schröger gave a slight bow. This was noted with approval by von Igelfeld, who saw the effect it had, and who resolved to bow to her himself when he next had the opportunity.

'So, you're the shrink,' said Pom Pom.

Dr Schröger laughed politely. 'How very amusing,' he said.

Pom Pom noticed that the psychiatrist was staring at the tattoo on her wrist, a small, delicately worked design of a dove ascending. She pulled back her cuff to expose it further. 'A dove,' she said, and added, 'The symbol of peace, as you know.'

Dr Schröger nodded, and then looked up. 'The symbolic potential of art is considerable,' he said. 'A small dove means a lot in itself. Combine it with an olive branch and its symbolic meaning becomes all the greater.'

Alice had been hovering on the edge of this conversation; now she joined in. 'How many countries use doves on their flags? Very few. But eagles – they're everywhere. Power; might; masculinity. But doves?'

Dr Schröger turned to her. 'You're so right,' he said. 'People don't realise how symbolism confronts us at every turn.' He paused. 'And the poor animals bear so much of it, don't they? Pigs are symbols of gluttony. Dogs symbolise loyalty. The fox stands for cunning.' He paused again, and then said, almost as if adding an incidental observation, 'Even the hedgehog has its symbolic role to play.'

This remark was addressed to Alice, but in so far as it attracted any reaction, this came from von Igelfeld, who stiffened. The name von Igelfeld meant, when literally translated, *hedgehog field*, as *Igel* was the German name of that small, spiky creature. Such names occur in many cultures: the Todds encountered in Scotland are all foxes of one stripe or another, as are those who in France are called *Renard*. People called Hogg, a common enough surname, are all pigs, if not in appearance or habit, then at least by historical association. Von Igelfeld was not as common as those names, but was as strong in animal associations. Now von Igelfeld found himself wondering whether this sudden reference to the hedgehog was in some way a sly dig at himself – an opening salvo in the engagement between hunter and prey. Could it have been intended, perhaps, to elicit some sort of disclosure on his part about his family and its origins – a reaction that might then provide this inquisitive psychiatrist with some material to consider?

Von Igelfeld was silent.

Still Dr Schröger did not look directly at von Igelfeld as he continued, 'Many people are surprised to see the iconographical references to hedgehogs,' he said. 'Yet the hedgehog is there, if one looks for him.' And here, almost

White Shoes – and a Disclosure

too discreetly to be noticed, he glanced in von Igelfeld's direction. 'In many paintings, the hedgehog represents wisdom.'

Pom Pom smiled. 'Wisdom? Rather a large task for a small creature like that.'

'Of course, there are other guardians of wisdom,' said Dr Schröger. 'We must not forget Minerva.'

'Sure,' said Alice.

Pom Pom now pulled her cuff back into position. Dr Schröger, who had been gazing at the dove tattoo, looked up. 'Forgive me,' he said. 'It is very rude of me. One should not stare at the body art of others.'

Pom Pom reassured him that she did not mind. 'Why have body art if one is not prepared to show it to others?'

Hearing this, Alice frowned. 'I'm not sure about that,' she said. 'Is a tattoo for *you* or for the gaze of another? I ask this only because I'm not sure of the answer.'

Von Igelfeld had something to say about this. 'Does one ask a question for oneself?' he said. 'Or does one ask it for others?'

Dr Schröger looked at him with curiosity. 'That's a very interesting question,' he said. 'I wonder whether your question – that is, your question about the question of whether one asks a question for oneself or others – was that question itself, do you think, asked for yourself, so to speak? What do you think, Professor von Igelfeld?'

Von Igelfeld hesitated. He had not expected to be

addressed directly by Dr Schröger, and he knew that he had to be cautious. This could be a trap – and they had not even sat down at the table yet. At last, he gave a response. 'Some questions are, of course, statements. That has been my experience, anyway.'

The others digested this. Then Dr Schröger said, 'It's also true that we already know the answer to many of the questions we ask,' he said. 'And, of course, there is the *hypophora*.'

Alice looked uneasy. Pom Pom closed her eyes.

'That is where you ask a question and immediately answer it yourself,' Dr Schröger explained. '*And who do you think found it? I did.* That's an example.'

Pom Pom opened her eyes. She saw that von Igelfeld was gazing at her. She allowed herself the faintest of smiles, and then looked away.

'There are many questions,' Dr Schröger now said, 'that have their origin in the memory of suppressed traumatic experience. I once had a patient who kept asking people the same question, time after time. He did not expect an answer, and so did not get one.'

'What was the question?' asked Pom Pom.

'It's rather complicated,' replied Dr Schröger.

Pom Pom waited, but there was no further explanation.

Von Igelfeld frowned. 'If somebody asked me the same question time after time, I would give an answer – any answer – just to stop him.'

White Shoes – and a Disclosure

Dr Schröger considered this. 'Do you not like being asked questions, Professor von Igelfeld? Is it ... *painful* to you?'

Von Igelfeld felt the back of his neck becoming warm. This person, this psychiatrist, had no right to ask him questions about how he felt about anything. He waved a hand carelessly. 'There are so many questions – how could anybody possibly answer them all?'

'That's true,' said Pom Pom. 'People who ask too many questions are told a lot of lies. We all learned that at school. Remember? *Ask no questions, be told no lies.* Remember?'

'Sure thing,' said Alice.

They went into the dining room for dinner. Von Igelfeld found himself seated exactly where, in an earlier note to Frau Unterholzer, he had asked to be placed. He was pleased with this, but wished that she had not said, in a loud voice, as they sat down: 'I've put you where you asked to be, Professor von Igelfeld.'

He winced, and threw a sideways glance at Pom Pom. She had not heard, he decided, and nor, he thought, had Dr Schröger, who had already sat down and was examining the placemat before him as if its design contained some important secret. Perhaps it did, thought von Igelfeld; perhaps our choice of placemats is every bit as revealing as everything else about us.

*

'I didn't sleep very well last night,' Dr Schröger remarked to von Igelfeld as the first course was served. And then, casually, he asked, 'Do you find you wake up at night?'

Von Igelfeld was careful. It was small talk, of course – the sort of remark one makes at a social occasion simply to get the conversation going. But he reminded himself that nothing Dr Schröger said could be assumed to be of no significance. This was how they got things out of you – they made innocent remarks, seemingly leading nowhere, and then suddenly you had said something that was of immense personal significance.

'Sometimes,' he said. 'But no more than anybody else, I think.' The words were carefully chosen, the message being *I am perfectly normal.*

'I had a rather bad dream,' went on Dr Schröger. 'I find that when I wake up after something like that, it's hard to get back to sleep – you'll know how it is.'

The warning bells sounded again. *You'll know how it is...* That was an invitation to admit to disturbing dreams – and then the next question, of course would be, *Tell me about these bad dreams.*

'Oh well,' said von Igelfeld. 'The point about dreams is that they stop when you wake up. That's always a consolation.'

'Hah!' exclaimed Dr Schröger. 'But does that mean that a dream's effect is limited? I don't think so, you know. Dreams cast a long shadow.'

White Shoes – and a Disclosure

'Perhaps,' said von Igelfeld. 'Perhaps not. I don't know much about dreams.'

That, it transpired, was a mistake, as Dr Schröger lost no time in seizing the opportunity it presented.

'You don't know much about dreams because you don't dream very much?' asked Dr Schröger.

Von Igelfeld did not reply immediately. Eventually he said, 'I think I dream probably just as much as anybody else. No more, no less.'

'But you do have *some* dreams,' pressed Dr Schröger. And then, in a moment of inadvertent transparency, he continued, 'Tell me about them. Any interesting ones recently?'

Von Igelfeld shook his head. 'I tend not to remember them. When I wake up, I do – but only for a very short time.'

Dr Schröger looked disappointed, but he was not going to be deterred. 'Does it annoy you that you don't remember your dreams?'

Von Igelfeld felt he was on safe ground now. 'A bit,' he replied. 'Not remembering a dream is like losing a message that somebody's sent you. It's a bit frustrating.'

'A message?' snapped Dr Schröger. 'Do you get regular messages?'

Von Igelfeld would not fall into that trap. 'No,' he said. 'I don't.' He paused, and then continued, 'I don't know if I should speak about this, but since you ask about messages, perhaps I should.'

Dr Schröger's eyes narrowed. He lowered his voice now.

There were several conversations going on at other places at the table, but he still did not want anybody else to hear what he had to say.

'You should feel quite comfortable speaking to me,' said Dr Schröger. 'What you tell me goes no further.'

Von Igelfeld looked up the table. Dr Schröger followed his glance.

'Our dear host and colleague,' von Igelfeld began, 'seems to believe that he is being sent messages.'

Dr Schröger drew in his breath. 'Are you suggesting ...' he began.

'Far be it from me to suggest anything,' said von Igelfeld. 'But I heard that he believed he had been sent a message – from goodness knows where – to the effect that I was behaving irrationally. Can you believe it? I couldn't. Of course it was all in his mind, poor man. Sometimes life can get very stressful for busy and successful people like poor Professor Dr Unterholzer, and they can lose contact with reality.'

Von Igelfeld thought: *That will serve Unterholzer for trying to prove that I was losing my reason. That will teach him the lesson he so richly deserves.*

Dr Schröger said, 'Let me get this straight: you say that he thinks that you are disturbed in some way, while all the time ...'

'While all the time,' said von Igelfeld, nodding his head in agreement. 'It is *he* who is disturbed – not seriously

White Shoes – and a Disclosure

disturbed, of course, but a little bit touched. There are many people in universities who are a little bit touched, I regret to say. Perhaps poor Professor Dr Unterholzer is in that company. Perhaps he is not. Who am I to tell?'

Dr Schröger became silent, and von Igelfeld turned now to face Pom Pom on his other side. She was tackling the soup they had served, trying to pick up a floating crouton with her spoon.

'This is artichoke soup,' Pom Pom said. 'It is a particular favourite of mine. Do you like it, Moritz-Maria?'

He told her that he did.

She managed to get the crouton onto the spoon. Then she went on, 'Of course, my favourite dish is gumbo. Have you heard of it? Gumbo. It's a big thing down where Alice and I live – New Orleans gumbo. Heaven on a plate.'

Von Igelfeld nodded politely. He had heard of gumbo, but was not too sure what went into it. 'It's seafood, I believe,' he ventured.

'It can be,' Pom Pom said. 'I suppose it's quite like bouillabaisse. But you can have it with sausage – it doesn't have to be seafood. You can put all sorts of things into it. Celery. Peppers. A lobster, if you've got one. You name it – in it goes.'

'Delicious,' said von Igelfeld. He wanted her to say: come with me, now, and we'll go down to New Orleans and have some gumbo. He would say yes – without the slightest hesitation. He would say, 'Oh yes, dear Pom Pomesque one, I am ready to go all the way to New Orleans *right now* and sit with you down there and listen to the croaking of the frogs and the lapping of the water. Oh, I am perfectly ready for that.'

Pom Pom put down her spoon and wiped her lips with her table napkin. 'Alice likes gumbo too. She's a big gumbo fan. If you're born in New Orleans – as she was – they say you have Tabasco sauce in your blood – a bit of nonsense, of course, like most of the things they say.'

Von Igelfeld asked, 'Do you and Alice make gumbo together in your house in New Orleans?'

Pom Pom smiled. 'We don't share, Alice and I.'

'Of course not,' said von Igelfeld. 'I just wondered whether you might cook gumbo and invite Alice round to sample it from time to time – that sort of thing.'

'I don't make it,' said Pom Pom.

'You buy it, then?'

Pom Pom shook her head. 'No, my husband makes it.'

Von Igelfeld stared straight ahead. He felt his heart do something within him that he had never felt before. Was this how it felt when one's heart stopped – when one's heart simply said: enough – no point in going on? Making a supreme effort, he managed to say, 'Your husband?'

There was not enough wind in his system for the words to emerge in intelligible form. Pom Pom frowned. 'What was that?'

'Your husband?'

She was matter of fact. 'Yes. John – my husband. Didn't I mention him before?' She glanced at von Igelfeld.

Von Igelfeld said nothing. He was still looking straight ahead.

'I met John when we were both graduate students in Baton Rouge – that's a place not far from New Orleans. That's where Louisiana State University is. He was doing research in hydraulic engineering. That's what he does, you see. We've got a lot more water down there than we can use, you see.'

'Oh.' It was all he could manage.

'Yes. You bet.'

Whole worlds can be ended with very few words.

There was a brief silence.

'You'd like John,' she said. 'He's a quiet man, but you get him in the right mood and he tells great stories.'

'Stories . . .'

'Yes. And he plays the guitar. He's teaching both of the kids to play, and they're not doing too badly.'

Von Igelfeld nodded. 'It is very useful to play the guitar. I like to hear the guitar.' That, of course, was not true. Von Igelfeld had no interest whatsoever in the guitar, but he had to say something – he had to fill the void that had suddenly appeared in his life. How foolish I have been, he thought. How foolish.

He became aware that Dr Schröger was saying something.

'Has Detlev Amadeus said anything to you?' he asked, his

voice lowered to not much more than a whisper. 'Has he said things that you thought were a bit strange?'

Von Igelfeld turned to him. 'There is nothing wrong with Professor Dr Unterholzer,' he said firmly. 'And now, will you please pass me the salt?'

You Should Look Your Best for the King of Sweden

At morning coffee the next day, Herr Huber was full of praise for the evening in all its dimensions. Had not von Igelfeld felt that the company was utterly engaging? Von Igelfeld assured him that he had. Had he not thought the soufflé Frau Unterholzer served as the second course was perfectly cooked? He had. Did he not think that it was courageous to serve a soufflé to that number of guests, when a slight delay in removing it from the oven could result in its collapse? He did.

Unterholzer basked in these reports of his social success. 'We don't entertain a great deal,' he said, waving a hand in a gesture of insouciance, 'but when we do, we like to get it right, Herr Huber. And, of course, it is very pleasant to hear that one's efforts are appreciated.'

Von Igelfeld sipped at his coffee. His memories of the evening were rather different, being dominated by the discovery that Pom Pom had a husband back in Louisiana. How could he have failed to entertain that possibility? he asked himself. Was he really that insensitive?

He thought back to their earlier meetings. As far as he could recall, she had said nothing about her domestic circumstances, and he had not really given the matter much thought. In so far as he had considered it, he had imagined that she might perhaps share a cottage somewhere with Alice, since they seemed to be such good friends and had interests in common – those motorbikes, for instance, and tattoos, not to mention Provençal literature. Now that he thought of it, he could just picture the two of them sitting on their porch, watching the Mississippi River slide past, perhaps sharing a bowl of that gumbo she had talked about. But that was not how it was, and now he had to come to terms with the fact that he had got it all wrong.

He sighed. It was not an audible sigh – not one that Herr Huber or Unterholzer, the only other people present, could have heard – but it was a sigh nonetheless. It was important not to allow disappointments to assume greater significance than they deserved. He had entertained hopes of a closer relationship with Pom Pom, but that was clearly not to be. He would be left, though, with fond memories that he could enjoy later on, after the two visitors had gone and everything had returned to normal. After all, to have had romantic feelings, even if they are unfulfilled, is better than not to have had any romantic feelings at all. What did Tennyson say? It is better to have loved and lost than never to have loved at all. That was so true, he thought, even if it was a pity that Tennyson said it rather than Goethe. He wondered whether Tennyson had got it from Goethe, and failed to acknowledge the source. Perhaps Goethe had *said* it, rather than written it, and then Tennyson had met somebody who reported that Goethe had spoken the line and Tennyson had incorporated it in his poem. That was perfectly possible, he thought: poets were always taking lines from other literatures and claiming them as their own.

Von Igelfeld gathered his thoughts. He would not allow what he now thought of as the *loss* of Pom Pom to weigh too heavily. He had endured disappointments before – indeed, in some respects all life was a disappointment – and he knew that he would soon get over it. After all, he was the author of *Portuguese Irregular Verbs*, and that still counted for something, even in a world of frivolity and superficiality. He had colleagues all over the world who knew his work and appreciated it. Look at Pom Pom and Alice – they had been drawn to Regensburg, he believed, because they knew of his work, and then there was Professor Fantozzi and his chapter – *entire* chapter – on his work in this recent volume, that he would read sooner or later, no matter how long Unterholzer tenaciously and inconsiderately held on to it. Yes, he had a lot to be grateful for, and he would not begrudge Pom Pom her domestic happiness back in Louisiana with that husband of hers and their children.

Lost in thought, he did not hear the question that

Unterholzer put to him. He looked up and apologised. 'I'm sorry, Professor Unterholzer, but I was thinking of something else.'

Unterholzer smiled – a tolerant, understanding smile. 'I imagine you have a great deal to think about, Professor von Igelfeld. But don't *brood*, whatever you do. Brooding does nobody any good.' He paused and gave von Igelfeld a slyly inquisitive look. 'What I wanted to ask was whether you had enjoyed meeting Frau Unterholzer's cousin last night.'

Von Igelfeld remained perfectly poised. 'A very charming man,' he said. 'Please tell Frau Unterholzer, Professor Unterholzer, that I found her cousin most agreeable company.'

'I am glad to hear that,' said Unterholzer. Then, after a moment or two, he continued, 'What did you talk about?'

Von Igelfeld hesitated. This really was too much. Not content with making an underhand arrangement to have von Igelfeld subjected to psychiatric examination, Unterholzer now sought to expose the details. It occurred to von Igelfeld that Unterholzer's whole ploy had, as he had hoped, misfired. Far from being prepared to be reveal to Unterholzer what he had elicited from von Igelfeld, Dr Schröger had probably refused to say anything, thereby tantalising Unterholzer as to what had been discovered. Von Igelfeld realised that he had muddied the waters by suggesting to Dr Schröger that Unterholzer himself was showing symptoms of mental disturbance, but he had, on second thoughts, very clearly rescinded any such suggestion. In that respect, his conscience was clear – unlike Unterholzer's, he imagined.

He answered Unterholzer's question. 'Various matters,' he said. 'We talked about this and that. Dr Schröger is a man of broad interests.'

Unterholzer's brow furrowed. 'It sounds as if you had a deep discussion,' he said.

'No,' said von Igelfeld. 'It was perfectly *normal*, Professor Unterholzer.' And added, almost as an afterthought, 'Not that one would imagine any conversation over your dinner table to be *abnormal*.'

Unterholzer had a tendency to flush red when flummoxed, and he did so now. This caused Herr Huber to enquire as to whether he was feeling unwell. 'I trust you are not unwell, Professor Unterholzer,' he said. 'Your colouring is a bit intense at present.'

Unterholzer said nothing, but glared at Herr Huber in a discouraging way. Herr Huber looked apologetic. He was a librarian, and he was aware that there were certain things that it was not for librarians to do. One of these was to pass comment on the appearance of professorial staff.

'I'm sorry,' Herr Huber stuttered. 'It's just that . . . '

Unterholzer waved the apology aside. 'I can assure you I'm quite well, Herr Huber,' he said. 'Your concern is unnecessary, but thank you anyway.'

It was an emollient response on Unterholzer's part, and Herr Huber inclined his head in gratitude, as might one who received a blessing from an ecclesiastical dignitary. For his part, Unterholzer decided that no further information was likely to be garnered from von Igelfeld. He finished his coffee quickly, spilling a few drops on his shirt front – as he often did. Von Igelfeld noticed this, as did Herr Huber: they had seen it many times before and had resisted the temptation to say anything, mainly because it was difficult to imagine what one might say in such circumstances. Von Igelfeld believed that the problem was caused by some sort of design fault in Unterholzer's chin, which sloped in towards his neck at an angle that seemed to invite such dribbling of liquids. Little could be done about remedying physical shortcomings, of course, but Unterholzer might still exercise a little bit more caution in the way he held his cup, for instance, and in the angle of approach adopted when drinking coffee. That, however, was not something that von Igelfeld thought he could suggest, as Unterholzer was always ready to take offence over the slightest matter – let alone in response to a direct and unambiguous comment on the topography of his chin.

Unterholzer left, and von Igelfeld decided to have a second cup of coffee. As he helped himself, Herr Huber remarked that the latest issue of the *Revue des Langues Romanes* had arrived in the library and that he had been perusing the contents. There was nothing unusual about that, of course: Herr Huber made a point of browsing through the journals so that he could draw the attention of von Igelfeld and the others to any new article that might be of interest to them.

This was appreciated, particularly by von Igelfeld when some reference was discovered to *Portuguese Irregular Verbs*.

Now Herr Huber said, 'I see that Professor Unterholzer is in the latest issue of the *Revue des Langues Romanes*. His paper is the lead item, in fact.'

Von Igelfeld lowered his coffee cup. 'Unterholzer?' he said. 'Lead item?'

'Yes,' said Herr Huber. 'They've printed his paper that won the Lafargue Prize. The French are so generous. It's twenty thousand Euros, would you believe? That's a lot of money – not as much as the Nobel Prize, of course, but perhaps Professor Unterholzer will be winning that next.' He paused, to smile broadly. 'Just imagine that. Imagine if Professor Unterholzer were to become a Nobel laureate! We would all go to Stockholm to witness the conferring of the prize. He'd have to wear white tie and tails, you know – that's the dress code for the Nobel Prize. He'd have to be a bit careful not to spill coffee on his shirt front – not if he was going to meet the King of Sweden. I gather that the Swedish monarchy is fairly informal, but there are still things that you would not want to do – such as to shake hands with the King while your shirt front has coffee stains on it. You wouldn't want that, I think.'

Von Igelfeld drew in his breath. This was a double blow – delivered without warning. 'You mean ...' He did not finish. It was too simply too much.

'Yes,' continued Herr Huber, seemingly unaware of von

Igelfeld's growing distress. 'I must show him the journal. There's an editorial at the beginning of it in which they talk about his paper and also comment on how well deserved the prize is.'

Von Igelfeld's mouth was set in a thin line of dismay. Now he said, almost through clenched teeth, 'You wouldn't be able to show it to me, would you, Herr Huber?'

The obliging Herr Huber said that this was perfectly possible, and offered to make a copy of the relevant pages and deliver them to von Igelfeld's office immediately after coffee. 'I had a quick look at the paper,' he said. 'I expect you'll find it interesting. It seems to involve considerable discussion of *Portuguese Irregular Verbs*.'

Von Igelfeld said nothing, but his mind was a turmoil of unanswered questions. What was Unterholzer doing writing about *Portuguese Irregular Verbs* without saying anything about it? Was it possible that his tone was so critical that he had not dared to mention the paper to him? And why had the judges of the Lafargue Prize given their *imprimatur* to a piece of work that must be, by its very nature, derivative? If anybody deserved the Lafargue Prize, it was him, and not Unterholzer, whose best work, such as it was, had been done at least ten years ago and who was very rarely quoted by anybody of status in the world of romance philology. Oh, the world was a misguided, superficial place – a place in which reputable scholarship was marginalised while superficiality and meretriciousness flourished unreproached.

He made his way back to his office where, a few minutes later, Herr Huber appeared with a photocopy of Unterholzer's paper in the *Revue des Langues Romanes*.

'I have copied the editorial, too,' he said. 'You will see that they have been most complimentary.'

Von Igelfeld thanked the Librarian and sat down at his desk to read the papers with which Herr Huber had presented him. He had barely progressed beyond the first paragraph when he felt himself choking with emotion. It was every bit as bad as he had feared – indeed worse. Unterholzer's paper, although purporting to be a critique of the ideas developed by von Igelfeld in *Portuguese Irregular Verbs*, was nothing more than their repetition, disguised in new language, but demonstrably the same as their original expression. And when he turned to the editorial in which the *Revue* misguidedly welcomed the award of the Lafargue Prize to Unterholzer, the sheer injustice of the situation all but overwhelmed him.

The world of Romance philology has reason to be grateful to Professor Detlev Amadeus Unterholzer, gushed the editors. *The ideas expounded in his groundbreaking paper, printed in this issue, cast a new and valuable light on the development of the Portuguese language from the fourteenth century to the present day. Professor Unterholzer has shone a light into obscure corners and illuminated a treasury of linguistic richness. His work will long stand as a model to be emulated by future generations of scholars.*

Von Igelfeld reeled. Unterholzer appeared to be saying nothing new in his article, which was entirely without merit as far as he could see. And here he was receiving the praise that was rightly von Igelfeld's: the sheer effrontery of this was breathtaking. It was no wonder that Unterholzer had said nothing about either the paper or the prize: only the most ruthless, the most meretricious, the most *shameless* could ever have brazened out this extraordinary act of academic hijacking – for that, von Igelfeld said to himself, is what it amounted to.

For a short while, von Igelfeld wondered how he should respond to this outrage. There was a case, he thought, for contacting Zimmermann immediately, and getting him to remonstrate with the editors of the *Revue* and, indeed, the organisers of the Lafargue Prize. At least Zimmermann would understand: he had consistently defended the traditions of German scholarship, and would be aware of people like Unterholzer and their machinations. A word from him in the right quarter might lead to a corrective editorial in a future issue of the *Revue* and could even result in the cancellation of Unterholzer's award. That would be a salutary lesson for him and one that would also discourage others from attempting such academic adventurism in the future.

He took a deep breath. Everything was going wrong – everything. He closed his eyes. Perhaps he should simply resign. Perhaps he should go off to live in the country somewhere and lead the life of a gentleman scholar, untroubled by the need to work with colleagues; not to have to deal with bureaucrats such as Herr Uber-Huber; not to have to listen to Herr Huber going on about his aunt and her nursing home and all the trivia that seemed to make up his world. He could do that if he wished, and even if they came to him on their bended knees, imploring him to return, he would reply, with quiet dignity, that his mind was made up and there would be no going back.

That would teach them. That would show those people at the *Revue des Langues Romans* that giving prizes to people like Unterholzer had *consequences*.

He opened the top drawer of his desk and withdrew a sheet of headed notepaper. *Professor Dr Dr* (honoris causa) (mult.) *Moritz-Maria von Igelfeld* announced the paper. Underneath this protestation, von Igelfeld wrote:

To His Magnificence, the Rector.

And beneath that,

Your Magnificence, It is my regretful duty to report to you my intention of resigning from the Institute of Romance Philology with immediate effect. I would not wish to leave you searching for an explanation, and so I should inform you that I take this step only because to remain would be unconscionable. Your servant, Moritz-Maria von Igelfeld.

That would give the Rector something to think about, thought von Igelfeld. He would panic of course, the poor man. He would quickly come up with increasingly attractive offers, perhaps dangling the prospect of several more assistants to add to the ones von Igelfeld already had. There were would be invitations to dinners and tickets to the opera, but von Igelfeld would turn them all down, at least to begin with. His mind was made up: the University of Regensburg could do what it might, but he would not budge. There were times when those who would never be accepted in the higher reaches of scholarship – and the Rector, after all, was undoubtedly one of those – were reminded of where they stood in the order of things.

He posted the letter in the University's private delivery system. That was at eleven-thirty. At eleven forty-two a reply came in:

Dear Professor von Igelfeld, Your resignation is accepted as from three p.m. today. The human resources department will be in touch to discuss the reallocation of your room, which we would be grateful if you could vacate by the time indicated above.

And it was signed, with astonishing bravado, by none other than Herr Uber-Huber, who claimed to be writing on behalf of the Rector.

Von Igelfeld had been smiling to himself. But now, the

smile became a frown. He had not expected this response. He had imagined that his letter would invoke a desperate plea from the Rector himself – a plea to which he himself would eventually yield with a certain graciousness. And now there was this peremptory request – no, *order* – that he should vacate his room. It was preposterous, and could not, under any circumstances, be abided. Picking up the letter, that he had, in his shock, allowed to fall onto his desk, he read it again. Then, in a sweeping movement that expressed the depth of his contempt for the likes of Herr Uber-Huber and, indeed, all bureaucrats, he tossed the piece of paper into the bin. Thus perishes all pettifoggery, thought von Igelfeld. He had always thought that if you ignored people like Herr Uber-Huber, they went away and you heard no more from them. There was no reason, he told himself, to believe that the outcome in this case would be any different.

Reallocate his room? The thought was outrageous. Reallocate? To *whom*, exactly?

Love in the Lives of Others

The throwing of Herr Uber-Huber's letter into the bin may have been cathartic for von Igelfeld, but its broader impact was, unsurprisingly, irrelevant. That very afternoon, shortly after the expiry of the three o'clock deadline for the vacating of his room, von Igelfeld heard a loud knock on his door.

He looked up in irritation. He discouraged afternoon callers, as it was the time in which he did some of his best work. At that precise moment he was reading the proofs of an important article he had written for a Hamburg-based journal, the editorial board of which was chaired by Zimmermann himself. It was not the sort of task that could be readily laid aside, and von Igelfeld prepared to give short shrift to whomsoever it was who had disturbed him.

It was Herr Uber-Huber, accompanied by a thin-faced woman administrator whom he introduced as Frau Wolfeschleghausen. Von Igelfeld had glimpsed this person from time to time, striding with some purpose about the University, but had never met her. Now he discovered from Herr Uber-Huber that she was the principal compliance officer of the University.

Von Igelfeld did not forget that he was at least the twelfth most identifiable bearer of the von Igelfeld name, and could not, therefore, be deliberately rude to anybody – even to somebody like Frau Wolfeschleghausen, or, of course, Herr Uber-Huber – no matter what provocation these intrusive bureaucrats offered.

'I would be delighted if you were both to sit down,' said von Igelfeld. 'Unfortunately, I am somewhat busy at present and it would be more convenient if we could meet some other time – perhaps next Thursday. Would that suit you, dear Herr Uber-Huber?'

Herr Uber-Huber glanced at Frau Wolfeschleghausen. She looked grave, and shook her head. In her thin face, von Igelfeld noticed, her sharp black eyes flashed.

'I'm afraid that will not be possible,' said Herr Uber-Huber. 'We need to make arrangements for this room. I gather that the colleague moving into it wishes to make the move as soon as possible.'

'Tomorrow morning, in fact,' said Frau Wolfeschleghausen.

Von Igelfeld stiffened. 'What colleague?'

'Professor Unterholzer,' replied Herr Uber-Huber.

'In accordance with the will of His Magnificence, the Rector,' offered Frau Wolfeschleghausen.

Von Igelfeld felt himself swaying. He reached out to steady himself, and his hand grasped the corner of the nearest bookcase. On that very shelf were several copies of *Portuguese Irregular Verbs*, standing like rocks in a fast-flowing and perilous stretch of the Rhine. They gave him the anchor he needed, the strength to fight against this monstrous intrusion.

'This is absurd,' he said.

'Not absurd,' said Frau Wolfeschleghausen, shaking a finger at him.

Von Igelfeld pretended not to see this gross impertinence. He opened his mouth to explain that he really needed to get back to work, but was distracted by the arrival of another visitor. This was Herr Huber, who had been passing by and had seen the two administrators standing in von Igelfeld's room. His instinct told him that help was needed.

Herr Uber-Huber spun round. 'Ah,' he said. 'It's you.'

Herr Huber looked towards von Igelfeld. He saw him holding on to the bookshelf for support. He saw the pained expression. He immediately understood. He might have been a librarian, but now he was a knight on his charger, ready to rally in support of the cause of all that was right and proper, and permanent. How dare this so-called Uber-Huber throw his weight around. *Uber*-Huber indeed – as if to be a mere Huber was not good enough. What next? *Mega*-Huber, perhaps.

'You must leave Professor von Igelfeld to get on with his work,' he said. 'If there are any matters that you would like to discuss with me, then I am available.'

Herr Uber-Huber was curt. 'Thank you, Herr Huber, but we do not require any assistance from you. If we encounter any library issues, rest assured that we shall avail ourselves of your advice.'

'Yes,' said Frau Wolfeschleghausen. 'You may go now.' And with that she shook a bony finger at Herr Huber.

This was too much for von Igelfeld. It was one thing for Frau Wolfeschleghausen to shake her finger at him – quite another to shake the same finger at poor Herr Huber, who was only a librarian, but who was nonetheless his brother-in-arms when it came to presenting a united front against the University administration.

Von Igelfeld made up his mind. Letting go of the supporting bookshelf, he drew himself up to his full height and fixed Herr Uber-Huber with a commanding stare. 'You must forgive me for leaving you,' he said. 'But I must go off immediately to see the Rector. His Magnificence is expecting me.'

At the mention of the Rector, Herr Uber-Huber hesitated. He looked anxiously at Frau Wolfeschleghausen, who looked anxiously back at him. 'Well ...' he stuttered, and then like the defenders of Jericho before Joshua's onslaught, he seemed to lose all will to resist.

Von Igelfeld sensed – and pressed – his advantage. Now to

Herr Huber he said, 'And Herr Huber, perhaps you would care to accompany me.'

Herr Huber nodded readily. 'I am at your disposal, Professor von Igelfeld.' And then, as a delicious aside, 'We must let Herr Unter-Huber ... no, forgive me, Herr Uber-Huber and Frau ... Frau Schnigelwolfenhauser ... get on with their work.'

It was a magnificent performance on Herr Huber's part, thought von Igelfeld. That would show these people. That would spike their feeble, bureaucratic guns.

Herr Uber-Huber did not stay. Turning on their heels, he and Frau Wolfeschleghausen left the room, under the glare of both von Igelfeld and Herr Huber.

'We shall indeed go to see the Rector without delay, Herr Huber,' said von Igelfeld. 'We should nip this nonsense in the bud, don't you think?'

Herr Huber allowed himself a smile. He had been waiting for months, if not years, to do something to put Herr Uber-Huber in his place, and now, at last, the opportunity presented itself. This was a blow for Hubers everywhere – for plain, unadorned Hubers, and indeed for librarians too, and he relished the thought of what lay ahead.

Together with Herr Huber, von Igelfeld presented himself at the reception desk in the University administration headquarters. The receptionist was polite, but made it clear that the Rector was extremely busy that day and would be unable to see them.

With an impatient move of his right hand, von Igelfeld brushed this objection aside. 'I, too, am busy,' he replied. 'But I have made time to see the Rector, and I am confident that he will make time for me. This is a matter of the utmost importance.'

The receptionist hesitated, and then picked up her telephone handset and spoke urgently into it. There was a short pause and then she turned and smiled sweetly at von Igelfeld. 'His Magnificence can spare fifteen minutes,' she said. 'A sudden window has opened up.'

Von Igelfeld thanked her, and then he and Herr Huber were led down a corridor to the Rector's office.

The Rector rose from his chair as his visitors entered.

'My dear Professor von Igelfeld,' he said. 'And my dear Herr Huber. This is indeed a great honour.'

They sat down. Then the Rector said, 'I was so sorry to hear of your resignation, Professor von Igelfeld, but there we are – nothing stays the same in the affairs of men, I always say.'

Von Igelfeld inclined his head briefly in recognition of the Rector's aphorism. 'Indeed, Magnificence. There is a constant flux in the affairs of men.'

'My thoughts entirely,' said the Rector. 'In the eyes of the gods, we mere mortals come and go.'

'Except that I am not going,' said von Igelfeld quickly. 'I have decided to stay after all.'

The Rector frowned. 'What a pity,' he said. 'I'm afraid it's too late, though. Oh, what a shame.'

Von Igelfeld waited.

'You see,' continued the Rector, 'if you were to stay, you would need to be reappointed, and we can't make any fresh appointments during the current academic year.' He paused, and adopted an expression of regret. 'Rules, you see, Professor von Igelfeld. Rules are the burden I bear in this life, but there we are.'

Von Igelfeld pursed his lips. 'But there are always ways round these things, Magnificence,' he said. 'I have never found rules to be so rigid as to prevent us from achieving the result we want.'

The Rector raised an eyebrow. He glanced at his watch. 'Such a pity,' he began, and then stopped. He was staring at von Igelfeld's right cheek.

Von Igelfeld shifted in his seat. Next to him, Herr Huber looked down at the floor – a picture of misery.

'Excuse my mentioning this,' the Rector began, his gaze still fixed on von Igelfeld's face. 'But I see you've had some sort of injury, Professor von Igelfeld.'

Von Igelfeld's hand went up to touch the plaster covering the scar he had received at the *Korps* meeting. 'Oh that?' he said casually. 'That's nothing.'

The Rector continued to peer at his cheek. 'One has to be very careful with any injury these days,' he said. 'Once these things get infected, it can be very difficult to deal with them.'

'I don't think there is any danger of that,' said von Igelfeld.
'How did you get it?' asked the Rector.
Von Igelfeld shrugged. 'One gets used to the occasional scrape as one goes through life,' he said.

The Rector frowned. 'But the position of that cut suggests ... '

He did not finish. Von Igelfeld raised a hand. 'I would not wish to mislead you,' he said. 'It is a duelling scar. I received it a few days ago in a duel I fought with a young man.' He wanted to add that in his view it was none of the Rector's business, but he decided not to say that. *Everything* could be the Rector's business, he thought.

The Rector was now sitting to attention. He was a man with a strong sense of the past – and respect for the upholders of tradition. And here, seated before him, was a man with links to ancient German academic traditions and who was, in addition, the bearer of a distinguished name.

'I'm sure we shall be able to do something,' the Rector now said. 'In fact, you may take it that your resignation is annulled, with immediate effect. Please disregard any communication to the contrary. All is restored to the position in which it was before any of these unfortunate misunderstandings occurred.'

Herr Huber looked up, his expression one of complete delight. Von Igelfeld was more restrained, but was clearly pleased. 'In that case, Magnificence,' he said, 'Herr Huber and I will trouble you no longer.'

'Oh, no trouble,' said the Rector magnanimously. 'And please pass on my good wishes to the members of the *Korps*.'

'I shall certainly do that,' said von Igelfeld.

'And you, Herr Huber,' said the Rector, turning to the Librarian. 'Please know how much I appreciate your efforts and those of your library staff.' He paused. 'I trust all is well with you.'

'Yes, it most certainly is,' said Herr Huber. 'I had a bit of a cold about a week ago – no, it must have been at least ten days, because it started the day that the Chancellor visited Bremen. I remember that very clearly because the papers had a picture of him talking to a local official who had exactly the same name as the manager of my aunt's nursing home – one Herr Sommer . . .'

'We really must go,' von Igelfeld interrupted. 'Come along, Herr Huber.'

There was a marked lightness in von Igelfeld's step as he made his way back to the Institute. Herr Huber accompanied him, but went off shortly after their return to inform Herr Uber-Huber in person of the outcome of their visit to the Rector. Von Igelfeld would have enjoyed doing this himself, but had agreed to let Herr Huber undertake the mission. 'I expect it will give you a certain amount of pleasure to do this, Herr Huber,' he said.

'It will,' said the Librarian. 'It is always good to be able to correct people who have an exaggerated idea of their own importance.'

'Oh yes,' said von Igelfeld. 'Such people are very trying to the rest of us.'

Herr Huber went off, and von Igelfeld settled back in his room. He looked about him, relishing the familiar surroundings that were no longer under threat. It would have been impossible to leave his office, he thought – he knew the position of every book on every shelf; he knew exactly where, in his copious filing cabinets, each off-print and photocopied article was carefully filed away. This was his world, and it was inconceivable that anybody else – Unterholzer in particular – could occupy it in his stead.

He returned to his task of working on the proofs for the Hamburg journal. Twenty minutes later, he was interrupted by another knock on the door. In normal circumstances, this would have irritated him, particularly since it came so hard on the heels of the unwanted visit by Herr Huber and Frau Wolfeschleghausen.

But this time it was Professor Pom Pom Boisseau.

'It's only me,' she said, as she came into the room.

Von Igelfeld sprang to his feet. Their romance was not to be, but in his eyes, Pom Pom was still surrounded by a warm glow.

'My dear Professor Boisseau,' he began.

'Pom Pom!' she scolded.

'My dear Pom Pom,' he corrected himself.

'I thought I might call on you just to see that everything was all right.'

Von Igelfeld invited her to sit down. 'Everything is very much all right,' he said. 'In fact, I'd go so far as to say that it is excellent.'

Pom Pom was pleased. 'It occurred to me that . . .'

She did not finish. 'There is no need,' interjected von Igelfeld. 'Everything, as I said, is perfectly all right.'

'Good,' said Pom Pom. She hesitated. 'In fact, I am the bearer of news that might add to that general sense of excellence.'

Von Igelfeld looked puzzled.

'I have heard from the Provost back at Tulane,' said Pom Pom. 'He sent me a message this morning to the effect that the University has resolved to confer on you an honorary degree – a doctorate of letters.'

Von Igelfeld closed his eyes. This was such news as he would never have dared dream. He had several honorary doctorates already, but there was always, always room for more. And a doctorate from Tulane University in New Orleans had a ring about it that far surpassed the degrees he already had. New Orleans . . . home of jazz, of Oysters Rockefeller, of gumbo . . .

He opened his eyes. Pom Pom was smiling at him. It seemed to give her as much pleasure to be the bearer of these tidings as it gave him to receive them.

'I am extremely honoured,' he said.

'And I hope that you will be able to travel to New Orleans to receive it,' Pom Pom went on. 'Alice and I will lay on a big party for you.'

'With gumbo?' von Igelfeld asked, and laughed.

'With gumbo and margaritas and a jazz band,' said Pom Pom. 'We'll have the girls from the motorcycle club and some people I know from the Quarter. *Le tout Nouveau Orleans* will be there, I promise you. And that will include my colleague who has been working on . . . '

'On the language of oysters?' asked von Igelfeld.

'Exactly,' said Pom Pom.

Von Igelfeld thanked her again.

Now a cloud passed over Pom Pom's face. 'I'm not sure how Professor Unterholzer will take it, of course. It would have been nice to be able to get an honorary doctorate for him too, but you know how it is . . . '

'Of course,' said von Igelfeld. 'There are minimum standards, I suppose.'

'Still,' said Pom Pom, 'it's good news about the Lafargue Prize, isn't it?'

Von Igelfeld hesitated, and Pom Pom noticed it. She looked at him. Very gently, she said something that she had been meaning to say for some time.

'You do know that he admires you,' she said, adding, 'In his very particular way.'

Von Igelfeld frowned. Unterholzer wanted to take his

room. He had conspired to have him declared insane. Did she know any of that?

'And sometimes,' Pom Pom continued, 'people respond in an odd way to the promptings of envy. And what we need to do in such cases is to let them know that we appreciate them. We need to make them feel better about themselves – especially . . . ' And here she seemed to weigh her words very carefully. 'Especially if we have so much ourselves.'

Von Igelfeld listened. Did he have as much as she seemed to suggest?

She answered the question for him. 'Your work is so widely appreciated. *Portuguese Irregular Verbs* is read throughout the world. You have been quoted in all the important works – even by Zimmermann.'

Von Igelfeld inclined his head in modesty.

'And now you have, or shortly will have, another honorary degree,' Pom Pom continued. 'Poor Professor Unterholzer has so little by comparison. Hardly anybody has ever read his book – Alice had never even heard of it, you know. And I started to read it, but didn't get beyond page forty-one.'

Von Igelfeld continued to listen.

'You know what I think you should do?' Pom Pom said. 'You should go to see Professor Unterholzer and tell him how pleased you are to hear the news of the Lafargue Prize. You might even say to him that you intend to write to Zimmermann to tell him about it.'

Von Igelfeld looked up at the ceiling. She was right. Pom

Pom was a good person – it was as simple as that. She was a good person who understood the workings of the human heart.

He drew in his breath. 'I think you're right,' he said.

'Sure I'm right,' said Pom Pom.

His eyes were drawn to her upper arm, just exposed by the short-sleeved shirt she was wearing. He saw a small tattoo – one that he had previously missed. He strained his eyes to see what it was.

It was a book, and in a moment of utter astonishment, he recognised its cover. It was a tattoo of *Portuguese Irregular Verbs*.

Pom Pom noticed his stare. She looked to her side, at the exposed tattoo. 'Oh that,' she said, blushing slightly. 'I hope you don't mind.'

Von Igelfeld shook his head. Of course he did not mind. He felt that he had so much in his life, and this was another thing to add to the list of blessings.

He did as Pom Pom suggested. Unterholzer was in his room, where he had just received the news from Herr Uber-Huber that he would not after all be moving into von Igelfeld's room. His disappointment was evident.

'I'm sorry I'm so late in congratulating you on the Lafargue Prize,' von Igelfeld began. 'It's such a richly deserved honour, Professor Unterholzer.'

Unterholzer struggled to grasp what he was hearing. But then he smiled broadly.

'You're very kind, Professor von Igelfeld.'

'And here's another thing,' said von Igelfeld. 'I think we should devote a future issue of the *Zeitschrift* to an appreciation of your work. A sort of retrospective, so to speak.'

Unterholzer stared at him. His eyes, which had a tendency to moisten, began to fill with what could only be tears. He took a handkerchief from his pocket and wiped at them. With tact, and in sympathy, von Igelfeld looked away.

'Thank you so much,' said Unterholzer.

They sat in silence. They had been colleagues for so long, and friends too. We must value old friends, no matter how from time to time they might test our patience. Von Igelfeld knew that; at heart he knew it.

Unterholzer raised a finger in the air, as if he had just remembered something.

'I have a book for you,' he said. 'I've been meaning to give it to you.'

It was the book that von Igelfeld expected it to be.

'It has a whole chapter devoted to you,' said Unterholzer. 'But that's no more than you deserve.'

'You're so kind,' said von Igelfeld. What Unterholzer said was probably true, but one would never make too much of it.

He returned to his room. The sky above was clear. The sky was Germany. A church bell rang somewhere, a sweet sound in the summer air. The bell was Germany. He saw two students walk past, hand in hand. It did not matter if there was not quite enough love in one's own life: what counted, he thought, was that there was enough love in the life of others.

Alexander McCall Smith is the author of over one hundred books on a wide array of subjects, including the award-winning The No.1 Ladies' Detective Agency series. He is also the author of the Isabel Dalhousie novels and the world's longest-running serial novel, *44 Scotland Street*. His books have been translated into forty-six languages. Alexander McCall Smith is Professor Emeritus of Medical Law at the University of Edinburgh and holds honorary doctorates from thirteen universities. He was knighted by the King in 2024.